difficult DEATH

René Crevel

Translated and with
an Introduction by
DAVID RATTRAY

North Point Press
San Francisco
1986

North Point Press
850 Talbot Avenue
Berkeley, California
94706

CONTENTS

FOREWORD

René Crevel offers a new bombshell in the genre of confrontation. Step right up for the rivalry between the hyperpassive zomboid posture of Surrealism and the lone-wolf, imperialist, paranoic-critical action program jesuitically fomented by none other than Salvador Dalí. The details of the intrigue that gradually led to André Breton's enthronement may seem otiose, but are by no means to be ignored, for Crevel does not exclude triviality from his position. Social fatality pursues its course. Nothing can save the victim, in this case, the Congress of Revolutionary Writers* at Kharkov, U.S.S.R. No doubt René Crevel retains the fact that poor old Hitler has got to be granted admittance to the Hall of Fame of the Irrational, but Breton's hatred of Hitler is outweighed only by his supreme and superficial benevolence toward the imminent cannibalisms of History.

The chief role is played by "the boredom of a country visit," the concatenation of circumstances culminating in the infernal machine of an approaching war. From this viewpoint, each detail has its importance. It is one more cog, one more piece in the jigsaw puzzle introducing the theme of fatality. "If God did not exist..." Is God the only way to escape this inexorable Fate no one is entirely responsible for, which is knocking blindly at the door?

Crevel is neither a mystic nor an atheist in the complete sense of his *Diderot's Harpsichord*. First of all, he insists on the revolutionary power of Poetry, which faith alone can inspire – faith in Man as an integral being, faith in a sort of aristocratic Anarchy which

* "Second International Congress of Revolutionary Writers," 1930.

vii

SALVADOR DALI

was the Anarchy of Prince Bakunin, "Prince" Rasputin, and which in a theatrical sense accommodates the painting of Tintoretto.

His dedication to Surrealism having, beyond the shadow of a doubt, required a strenuous psychic effort, René Crevel squandered his strength. The nature of his genius, as much as the gravity of his state, inclined him to the sweet and simple resolution he adopted in the end. Suicide. René! He seemed to regret leaving the vistas opening to him at every turn along the way to the gates of Knowledge. Often he turned to contemplate that portal in the mingled glow of sunset and the rising moon. With a sweet melancholy, he savored the poetry of the dying day. Perhaps he hoped to wear out his heart on these tender admirations in the same way he was burning out his brain and mind in a never-ending series of intellectual chores, making the most of a name that of itself predetermined in him the sequence of birth-death cycles that was to end only with his suicide.

★
★ ★

To start at the beginning, I must give a brief account of the A.E.A.R. The initials stand for Association des Ecrivains et Artistes Révolutionnaires (Association of Revolutionary Artists and Writers), a string of words that has the merit of signifying nothing much. Surrealism was at that time animated by a great gush of idealistic generosity. The Surrealists were also drawn to the ambiguous name of the thing, and so joined as a group, thereby constituting a majority in that association of middle-ranking bureaucrats. Like all associations of this type, the A.E.A.R. was doomed to vanish without a trace. Innately lacking, congenitally defective, as it was, its first official act was to call an "International Congress." Although I was the only one to denounce it in advance, the whole aim of this Congress was to liquidate all artists and writers of the slightest merit, especially those who might have claimed anything like a subversive and therefore truly revolutionary attitude. Congresses are strange monsters, naturally surrounded by smoke-filled rooms in which there is a constant flow of physiologically

viii

FOREWORD

adapted life-forms in which flexibility is the name of the game. Now, Breton is any number of things to any number of people, but number one, he is a man of integrity and hard-edged as a St. Andrew's Cross. No matter what the Congress, or whom its smoke-filled back room may contain, especially in fact if the said back room is a Congressional one, Breton instantly becomes the most obstructive and impossible to assimilate of "foreign bodies." He is constitutionally incapable of going with the flow or melting into the woodwork. This very fact was the main reason the Surrealist crusade never got one foot in the door at the Congress of the Association of Revolutionary Artists and Writers. It all came about exactly as I had quite astutely foretold without the slightest cerebral effort of any sort on my part.

The only member of our group to believe in the usefulness of a Surrealist participation in the International Congress of the A.E.A.R. was René Crevel. An extraordinary and deeply significant detail about Crevel is that he did not choose to be called Paul or André like Tom, Dick, or Harry, or even, like me, Salvador. Just as in Catalan the names Gaudi* and Dalí mean "to have an orgasm" and "to desire," respectively, Crevel's given name was René, which might well come from the past participle of the verb renaître, to be reborn, related to renascence. At the same time, he retained Crevel as his family name. Now the verb crever implies the act of kicking the bucket, croaking, dying – or, as linguistically minded philosophers would put it, "the élan vital of croaking." René was the only one to believe in the A.E.A.R.'s possibilities. He made it his launching pad. He became its fervent advocate. He was en-dowed with the morphology of an embryo, or rather (to be even more precise) the morphology of a fern frond at the moment it be-gins to open out and unfold the spirals of its nascent tendrils. You have yourself before now doubtless observed the sullen, deaf, Beethovenesque, bad-angel face of a fern shoot. If you have not yet given it too much thought, now is the time to think it over, and you will get a precise idea of what dear René Crevel's protuberant

* The architect-inventor of the Mediterranean Gothic style, who designed the unfinished Church of the Holy Family, a park, and many apartment houses in Barcelona.

retarded baby-face was apt to look like. At such times, he represented for me the most living symbol of Embryology. Today he is also transmuted in my eyes into the quintessential embodiment of this very new science titled Phoenixology, about which I am going to write a few words for all of you who are lucky enough to be reading me. It is likely that you still know nothing about it, which is a shame, for Phoenixology teaches those of us who are as yet among the living the marvelous chance we have of becoming immortal in the course of this life here on earth, thanks to the secret possibilities that we all possess of recovering our embryonic state and of thereby being literally born again over and over from our own ashes as was the Phoenix, that mythic bird whose name serves to baptize this brand-new science which bids fair to become the most special of all of today's very special sciences.

No one ever "creveled," that is, croaked so many times in quick succession, nor was anyone ever subject to so many rené-esque renascences as our own René Crevel. René spent his entire life in and out of hospitals. He was admitted half dead (crevé) only to be released reborn (rené), flourishing, shining, euphoric as a newborn babe. It never lasted. The self-destructive frenzy soon returned. He went back to suffering and smoking opium and tackling insoluble ideological, moral, æsthetic, and emotional problems. He indulged in insomnia and tears until they half killed him. Then he'd stare at himself, like the compulsive that he was, in all the mirrors for manic-depressives in the Proustian Paris of the day, repeating, "I look as if I were about to croak, I do think I am about to croak," until, at the end of his rope, he admitted to a few of his nearest and dearest, "I would rather croak than keep going one more day like this." So he'd get put in a "detox." Then, after several months of assiduous treatment had ensued, René was born again, and the whole thing would start over. We'd see him pop up in Paris, overflowing with life like a joyful child, dressed like a superior gigolo, dazzling, with a super permanent wave, and already in the throes of an optimism that unfolded freely in acts of revolutionary generosity; and so it went for a time, but then, once more, gradually, but there was no getting

FOREWORD

away from it, he was back on the opium, beating up on himself again, twisting himself out of shape like a nonviable fern shoot.

René spent his most rigorously euphoric furloughs from the "croak" side of his name and nature in that Port-Lligat that has long deserved to be immortalized by a Homer but merely belongs to Gala and me. These were the best months of his life, as he himself said in his bread-and-butter letters. Staying with us gave him a new lease on life. My asceticism made a deep impression. The whole time René was our guest at Port-Lligat, he lived like an anchorite in imitation of me. He got up in the morning before me, before the sun, and spent long days stark naked in the olive grove, face to face with the harshest, most lapis-lazulian sky in the whole of the Mediterranean, the most meridionally extremist of skies, in a Spain that was already dying of extremism. René loved me more than anybody else; but he loved Gala even more. Like me, René called her The Olive, and would say that if there wasn't a Gala, an Olive, that he could call his very own, life could only end in tragedy for him. It was at Port-Lligat that René wrote his books *Putting My Foot in It* (Les pieds dans le plat), *Diderot's Harpsichord* (Le clavecin de Diderot), and *Dalí and Anti-Obscurantism* (Dalí et l'antiobscurantisme). One day recently, Gala was looking back, comparing René with certain youthful figures of the present day. "They don't make boys like him any more," she pensively exclaimed.

Anyhow, once upon a time there was this thing called the A.E.A.R. Crevel was starting to look positively alarming. He thought he could find nothing better than the Congress of Revolutionary Artists and Writers to indulge in a barrelful of gruelingly aphrodisiac excesses of ideological agony and contradiction. As a Surrealist, René honestly believed that without making concessions we would be able to march in step with the Communists. However, long before the opening of the Congress, the vilest intrigues and the most craven denunciations were set working to guarantee the pure and simple liquidation of the ideological platform occupied by our group. Crevel, shuttling to and fro between Communists and Surrealists, throwing himself into a succession of wearisome and despairing attempts to conciliate the two, moved back and forth between "crevel" and "rené" as if caught in a revolving door between death and rebirth. Each evening brought new drama, new hope. The worst drama of them all was the final break with Breton. With tears in his eyes, René cried on my shoulder like a baby. I refrained from encouraging him in the Communist path. To the contrary, I employed my customary Dalinist tactic of provoking the maximum number of hopeless antagonisms in each and every situation so as to squeeze a maximum of irrational juice out of them all. At that moment, my "Lenin-grand piano-William Tell" obsession was beginning to lift and give way to that of the "edible-paranoid-great man," namely Adolf Hitler. To Crevel's tears, I replied that the only workable conclusion the A.E.A.R. Congress could come to would be to pass a motion declaring Hitler's soft eyes and curvaceous fanny possessed of an irresistible poetic charm, a declaration that need in no way preclude the struggle against Hitlerism on the political level, quite the contrary. At the same time, I confided to Crevel my doubts relative to the canon of Polycletus* and concluded that I was virtually certain that Polycletus was a fascist. Crestfallen, René took leave of me. Because he had had daily proofs of it during his stays at Port-Lligat, Crevel was of all my friends the only one who was completely convinced that at the bottom of my most truculent extravaganzas there was always a residue of (as Raimu put it) Truth. A week went by, and I felt a sudden sharp pang of guilt. I must phone Crevel, otherwise he would think I had been won over to Breton, although the latter was as far as the Congress itself from sharing my Hitleresque flights of fancy. During that week of waiting, the smoke-filled room had pushed all the buttons necessary to make it impossible for Breton to even read off the Surrealist group's report at the Congress. Paul Eluard was given the chore of presenting a version in place of Breton's. (Eluard's version, incidentally, was completely sugar-coated and watered-down.) After those days, Crevel must have felt perpetually torn between his duties as a Commu-

* Polycletus of Sicyon, Greek sculptor of the 5th century B.C.

FOREWORD

nist party member and the demands of Surrealism. When I finally did make the call, an unknown voice answered with Olympian disdain at the other end of the line: "If you're a buddy of Crevel's, find a cab and get over here. And make it snappy, he's dying. He tried to kill himself."

I leaped into a taxicab. Arriving in his street, I was amazed at the crowd. A firetruck was parked in front. I failed to grasp the connection between the firemen and the suicide. My first reaction (by a typical Dalinist association) was to imagine that suicide and fire had joined forces in the same building. I entered Crevel's bedroom jammed with firemen. With the gluttony of a nursing baby, René was sucking oxygen. I never saw anyone cling so desperately to life. After having done himself in on the Paris city gas, he was trying to be reborn on the oxygen of Port-Lligat. Attached to his left wrist was a cardboard slip, on which he had himself written in neat capital letters: RENE CREVEL. Because at that time I was still not altogether comfortable making phone calls, I rushed to the home of Vicomte and Vicomtesse de Noailles. They had been great friends of Crevel's. From their house I was enabled, with maximum tact and a modicum of style, to announce the news that was to stun Paris, news I had been the first to know. In the drawing room glittering with gilded bronzes, against a black and olive-green backdrop of Goya canvases, Marie-Laure de Noailles pronounced a few words on Crevel that were so inspired that they were instantly forgotten. Jean-Michel Franck, who was himself to commit suicide only a short time afterwards, was more shocked by Crevel's death than anyone, and had several anxiety attacks over the next few days. The night following, we went for a walk on the boulevards and ended up seeing a film on Frankenstein. Like every film I ever attended, it was true to my paranoia-critical system and illustrated Crevel's obsession with death down to the minutest necrophiliac details. Frankenstein even resembled Crevel physically. The whole film centered on the theme of death and rebirth and was thus something of a pseudo-scientific fore-taste of our brand-new science, Phoenixology.

The mechanical realities of the War were to sweep away ideological agonies of all sorts. Crevel was one of those fern shoots that can unfurl only at the edges of the brightly convoluted, Leonardo-like eddying depths of the fishponds of Ideology. Since Crevel, no one has had anything of substance to say about Dialectical Materialism, or Mechanical Materialism, or anything else for that matter. But Dalí hereby announces that when men's minds shall have rediscovered their best-chiseled ornaments, and that day is coming very soon, the words "Monarchy, Mysticism, Morphology, and Nuclear Phoenixology" will once more stir their hearts.

René Crevel, it's me calling you! Hey Crevel, wake up! To this, ever in the Spanish manner, you reply in Castilian: "Présenté!"

Salvador Dalí
(1954)

INTRODUCTION

In 1977 the art historian Gert Schiff lent me his copy of *La mort difficile* by René Crevel on the same day a big Brassaï show was opening at the Marlborough. Crevel I had heard of, thanks to an essay by Ezra Pound, "René Crevel," published in the English magazine *Criterion* in 1938. According to E. P., Crevel was the best of the post-World War One generation in France, although mainly unrecognized by his compatriots, and too bad for them: "A nation which does not feed its best writers is a mere barbarian dung heap..." I had never gotten around to reading him, though, nor had anyone else I knew, apart from Gert Schiff. But of course everyone is conversant with flapper-era Paris By Night as captured by Brassaï. It's a classic. Lovers in a café at dawn. Sleepy petulant sailors with bee-stung lips. Transvestites at the drag ball. Tweedy opium-smoking dowagers. On my way home from the show, I opened *La mort difficile*. Out popped a cast of characters very like those in Brassaï's photos. Within a short time, I found myself like Charlie Chaplin on the conveyor belt in *Modern Times*, being translated from hilarity to consternation, in other words, to the grind of transposing that experience into my own language under a new title: *Difficult Death*.

I had never met with the likes of René Crevel anywhere. Consider his description of the moment of falling in love:

> Hands pressed against hands, palms wedded palms. Pierre shuddered and then was nothing but a droplet of blood transfused into another life's bloodstream. Little by little, he altogether ceased to exist.

Or, on a more mundane level, the experience of finding oneself trapped at an avant-garde event in a gallery or performing space or loft in a great city of the 20th century. Let's say you are boxed in with a galaxy of break dancers and graffiti writers in the New York City of 1985. Here is Crevel's 1926 equivalent:

> Having invited a handful of snobs to watch a couple of juvenile delinquents bump and grind to the sound of a pianola, they imagined themselves to be prophets.

Similarly, take Crevel's observations on various individual sorts of people and their psychologies. For example, his characterization of someone who had "a special way of walking that could never quite help turning very rapidly into a dance" as a person who "fit inside his ego as naturally as an orange in its rind; never uncomplicated but always harmonious." Or his remark about Diane, heroine of *Difficult Death* who has made up her mind to remain a virgin forever – She doesn't know that ignorance of the joys of love makes them easier to give up. Quite possibly Saint Augustine beat Crevel to the punch on this one. It's so true, though, that it can't be repeated too often.

For years I wondered what the French see in us Americans. Not until I read Crevel's characterization of the American Arthur Bruggle in *Difficult Death* did I ever find the whole thing summed up in just a few words:

> The power that is Bruggle's has nothing to do with intelligence in the European sense of the word. Come up out of the depths of his being, Arthur's is a potency transcending all means of conscious self-expression, and it would be both unjust and inexact to speak of cunning with regard to him, but a mysterious energy bursts out of him like electricity from a cat's fur. A feline floating in a baggy jacket, a feline with big shoes ("The French," he says, "love shoes, not feet, clothes but not bodies, and that's why they live in such narrow, velvet-and-leather-lined rooms!"). Arthur, lost in his raglan overcoat, with each of his gestures puts one in mind not so much of all the hard work and study implicit in the elasticity of his movements as of the very instincts that predetermined the nature and direction of that study.

INTRODUCTION

There was another Bruggle in Crevel's first novel, *Detours*. In *Detours*, Bruggle is an American member of France's gilded youth who is capitalizing on his magnetism and good looks to eat, drink, and fuck his way through a world very similar to that portrayed in Raymond Radiguet's exactly contemporary *Count d'Orgel*. Like the Bruggle of *Difficult Death* (and the actual person he was based on, the American painter Eugene MacCown who was the love of Crevel's life), this Bruggle is bisexual. In Crevel's parlance, this term denotes a male homosexual who occasionally sleeps with a woman, one who

> if he was still capable of being aroused by a woman's warmth, it was more in response to the warmth than to the woman.

Predisposed to misogyny by a murderous relationship with his mother, Crevel was to succeed more than once in breaking out of the confining fear of the opposite sex, only to fall back into it soon after. His manifesto of bisexuality in *Putting My Foot in It*, where he boasts of having "fornicated with both sexes of the species and even several dogs," uncovers a deep streak of morbid fear and hostility. In vain he disguises it as just one more item on the agenda for social and intellectual liberation:

> Do you view erotic activities as subversive? Do you support the rebellion of the reproductive instincts against their preordained function?

The undercurrent remains one of anger against women for representing a stifling conformity to preordained function, leading to home, family, and responsibilities.

Crevel suffered from a very deep ambivalence about homosexuality itself. This ambivalence informs every page of his books where the subject comes up, and there are many. *Difficult Death* contains several pæans to cruising as a mystic communion and release, including Crevel's "anonymous continent" image, which occurs in virtually all of his books. But other passages in *Difficult Death* picture cruising as a descent into hellish degradation. In one instance, the anonymous encounters of men in dark doorways are fervently described: "...the body leaps, flies, weighs no more than a song under the midnight sun," and in another the protagonist castigates himself as one who "calls himself a man and is in fact nothing but a child in the grip of a nightmare." Of his lover MacCown, Crevel wrote in a letter to Marcel Jouhandeau: "He was sent to punish me by the people I have hurt."

Although at the time of writing Difficult Death Crevel was not yet "official," he had been involved with Eugene MacCown for a couple of years, while actively cruising on the side. He never made any effort to hide it from friends. This took courage. Most of Crevel's fellow Surrealists, including especially André Breton, were if anything rather more homophobic than your average middle-of-the-road Frenchman of that era. From 1921, when they first became acquainted, up until the final hours of René's life, in mid-June 1935, Breton was to loom large for Crevel. From start to finish, Crevel's behavior toward Breton exhibited a remarkable mix of timidity and intransigence. I have seen the inscription to Breton, in Crevel's hand, on a copy of his pamphlet Mind Against Reason, which is arguably a more powerful exposition of Surrealism as a philosophy than anything Breton himself ever wrote. This inscription meekly assures Breton that he and Crevel are "for and against the same things," although Crevel never once backed down on the issue of homosexuality. That same year, 1928, Breton published the following statement in his magazine Surrealist Revolution: "I accuse the homosexuals of affronting human tolerance with a mental and moral defect that tends to advocate itself as a way of life and to paralyze every enterprise I respect. I make exceptions, one of which I grant to the incomparable Marquis de Sade." One must assume that a similar exception was graciously extended to René Crevel. Difficult Death was a risky book to put forward in 1926 because it was a public statement of the author's ambivalent sexuality. Now, in 1985, Difficult Death is a risky book because of the author's disregard of received ideas on the subject, of ordinary prejudices attached to it, combined with a bone-deep honesty in his disclosure of his own feelings and experiences. Honesty of that order threatens Order. It's a security risk; and as

INTRODUCTION

Crevel observed in *Mind Against Reason*, there is nothing in this world that intellectuals dislike so much as risk.

The risk-taking that leads up to the suicide in *Difficult Death* has one thing in common with the audacities and failures that led to Crevel's own suicide, and that is that neither has anything to do with sexual problems. In 1925, the year Crevel was writing *Difficult Death*, *Surrealist Revolution* canvassed its contributors on the question, "Is Suicide a Solution?" Crevel responded:

A solution? Yes.

People say one commits suicide out of love, fear, or venereal disease. Not so. Everyone is in love, or thinks they are. Everyone is frightened. Everyone is more or less syphilitic. Suicide is a means of conscious choice. Those who commit it are persons unwilling to throw in the towel like almost everyone else and repress a certain psychic feeling of such intensity that everything tells you you had better believe it is a truthful and immediate sense of reality. This sense is the one thing that allows a person to embrace a solution that is obviously the fairest and most definitive of them all, the solution of *suicide*.

There is no love or hate about which one can say that it is clearly justified and definitive. But the respect (which in spite of myself and notwithstanding a tyrannical moral and religious upbringing) I have to have for anyone who did not timorously withhold or restrain that impulse, that mortal impulse, leads me to envy a bit more each day those persons who were hurting so intensely that a continuing acceptance of life's little games became something they could no longer stomach.

Human accomplishment is not worth its weight in horse mucus. When personal happiness leads to even a modicum of contentment, this is more often than not a negative thing, like a sedative taking effect. The life I accept is the most fearful argument against me. The death that tempted me several times was lovelier by far than this downright prosaic fear of death that I might also quite properly call a habit, the habit of timidity.

I wanted to open a certain door, and I got cold feet. I feel I was wrong not to open it. I not only feel, I believe, I want to feel, I want to believe it was a mistake not to, for as I have found no solution in life, notwithstanding a long and diligent search, I am not about to attempt to pull myself together to give life another try unsolaced by the thought of this definitive and ultimate act in which I feel that I have caught a glimpse at least of the solution.

DAVID RATTRAY

"The life I accept is the most fearful argument against me." In the 1920s French publishers used to tuck a loose insert in a book, containing the blurb and author's biography, stuff one sees on the back cover nowadays. For the blurb that came with *My Body and Me*, Crevel wrote his own bio, and it characterizes him in words he was to repeat almost verbatim in his portrait of that minor figure named Lucas in *Difficult Death* who is remarkable in that (apart from young Diane, who is Pierre's alter ego, good angel, and twin sister) he is the only decent person in the book. Of Lucas, Crevel says:

> He had never yet had the grace to change fads with every changing season, nor to share, according to the taste of the day, his contemporaries' enthusiasm for opium dens, Oxford trousers with outsized cuffs, and dance clubs of so-called ill fame.

Of himself, in the blurb, Crevel writes:

> Hates fads, be it the mystique of Oxford University and trousers with outsized cuffs, or that of movie palaces and related funhouses, Negroes and jazz, music halls, and player pianos.

Yet Crevel spent half his life smack in the middle of all that. The blurb continues:

> In search of characters for future novels, men and women naked and alive as knives and forks, to figure in tales as unprintable as the ones he used to make up when he was a little kid.

This shows Crevel was already mulling *Babylon* over in his mind, with its famous opening chapter, "Mr. Knife, Miss Fork," a good two years before he actually wrote it. More importantly, the image of "men and women naked and alive as knives and forks" conjures up a vision of a new humanity, of people as clean and sparkling and smooth and hard and shapely and bright and tuneful and functional as so much good silver. Further: it suggests simplicity and candor. Qualities that contradict what he referred to as "the life I accept," in his statement on suicide. Crevel disliked trendiness of all sorts, regardless of social or sexual markings, but the Surrealist camp of which he was a leading ideologue represented an apotheosis of camp, camp for camp's sake, and the

INTRODUCTION

Surrealist association with the world Communist movement was preposterous – as only Dalí seems to have had the wit or the sense of humor to grasp at the time. Bear in mind that the René Crevel who was caught up in all this was the same guy who "intended to give all his attention to an immediate sense of reality" (Breton's words in discussing the motives of his suicide). A striving to capture and share that "immediate sense of reality" against all odds is present in all of Crevel's writings. By the summer of 1935, Breton says, Crevel was in despair "at not being physically able to maintain himself at that level." What is meant by the phrase "not being physically able"? Incurable pulmonary disease, hereditary syphilis, plus liquor and drugs. But there was something more at the end. This I heard from Gert Schiff; it forms part of an unpublished interview he had some years ago with the art historian and founder of the French Museum of Modern Art, Jean Cassou, who was an eyewitness. It's nothing much, actually. Just that Crevel made an appearance during those last days in front of a working-class audience, giving a talk on Art and Love and Revolution, subjects about which he supposed himself to be on common ground with his listeners. This was not Crevel's debut as a lecturer. Already a decade earlier, when *La mort difficile* was first published, in 1926, Crevel had given such a talk in London. The event was described by the critic Logan Pearsall Smith:

> All the young lions, or rather the young tom-cats of Bloomsbury were there, a few older celebrities, trembling for their thrones and reputations among those hoping to replace them, and a few ladies of fashion anxious to be in the intellectual swim. This audience was addressed by a pert, self-confident French boy with a big mouth and a brazen voice [Crevel] who dinned our ears with a galimatias of what I thought pretentious and incomprehensible nonsense, a new gospel of *sur-réalisme* composed of Freud, Rimbaud, Valéry, Keyserling and Mussolini – an anti-intellectual gospel and attack on reason, chanted and bellowed at us in a kind of figurative and bombastic prose which, though we pretended to follow it, I am sure none of us really understood. The whole thing – the brazen pretentious boy and the anxious pretentious audience – was extremely funny.
>
> (Letter to Cyril Connolly, dated Autumn 1926.)

DAVID RATTRAY

Unlike the bright young things of 1926, the workers of 1935 were unimpressed. The talk was a flop. Here, considering the lifelong thirst for reality that was Crevel's, I see a thread leading straight to the final chapter. To understand what happened in the question-and-answer period that followed the talk, it is necessary to have some idea of how Crevel viewed himself up to that moment. Over the past decade he had grown accustomed to thinking of himself as a poet, a witness of the truth, an "unacknowledged legislator." The world, at least a sophisticated segment of the reading public, had recognized him in that role. His view of himself as a poet rather than a novelist, even though his published writings consisted almost entirely of fiction and essays, reflected an allegiance to Surrealist literary theory, which had it as a basic tenet that the old genres were finished, and all that remained for a writer in today's world was the pamphlet and poetry, on the writing front, at least.

Pamphlets. In other words, philosophy and criticism in the service of a worldwide Communist revolution. To actual Communist party members, then as now, the Surrealists' efforts along those lines, including Crevel's, were a laugh. Crevel's essays certainly do cut a bizarre figure if viewed as contributions to Marxist-Leninist theory. *Diderot's Harpsichord* and *Mind Against Reason* present the most powerfully argued defense of the irrational since Nietzsche; and the essays on Klee, Sintenis, and Dalí reveal a critical eye of penetration and originality linked with an extraordinary breadth of historical perspective. Anna Balakian has written that Crevel would have been the philosopher of Surrealism had he survived. These five pamphlets, actually booklength essays, represent the unfulfilled juvenilia of that philosopher.

Poetry. Crevel believed in the programmatic restriction to pamphlets and poetry and conformed to it in his own way, as a poet, in that his novels are not novels so much as they are richly poetic discourses with elements of narration and a storyline. The novella *Detours*, his first book, was an exception (which Breton returned to Crevel without comment, while other members of the Surrealist group marveled at his temerity in asking Breton to read it in the first place). The other five – *My Body and Me* (1925), *Difficult Death* (1926), *Babylon* (1927), *Are You Crazy?* (1929), and *Putting My Foot in It* (1933) – have much more in common with Richard Pryor than with Marcel Proust. According to Klaus Mann's recently republished memoirs, Crevel was in the habit of electrifying friends with raps very similar in style to his novel-writing. The manner varies from rapid narration to slapstick and beyond, to lyric flights with a shapeliness of the language itself that adds up more to a storyteller-poet than a poetic storyteller. Present tense and indicative mood predominate from start to finish, creating a myopic closeness to the details of what is being stated or told similar to that which characterized the cinéma vérité of the 1950s and again the structuralist film of the Sixties and Seventies.

The whole point of all this was to communicate an immediate sense of the reality and life that is right at hand for every one of us the moment we exercise our freedom to reach out for it and live it in our own minds and bodies: "Poetry is the highroad of freedom." Crevel used a couple of analogies to illustrate this slogan: "A contemporary of Diderot's imagined a color harpsichord; Rimbaud in the *Sonnet of the Vowels* revealed the prism of sounds; Poetry bridges the gaps between our senses, between image and idea, idea and precise fact." A color harpsichord, a prism, a spark. What they have in common is that all three are mediums. Sometime in 1921 Crevel had obtained initiation as a medium. He in turn initiated Breton in the experiments with hypnosis and automatic writing that were to open up the dark continent of the unconscious to the Surrealists. The barriers separating the unconscious from the conscious mind, dream from reality, had long been perceived to be chief among the walls that hem life in, and it is thanks to Crevel that Surrealism developed the techniques that it did for breaking down those walls with a view to realizing, if only in some small measure, Rimbaud's brave program to "change life."

To avenge herself on a faithless husband in the year 1903, Madame Crevel had had little René circumcised at the age of three, an event that was to burn henceforth at the center of his mind in images of sperm and blood, an obsession the Pythago-rean teachings associate with the condition of a soul wavering on the brink of a fresh descent into material existence. The ancients pictured such unborn souls as brides of Neptune, sea nymphs hovering in a white mist over the flood of materiality: "They are in love with blood and semen, just as the souls of plants are nour-ished by water." (Porphyry, *On the Cave of the Nymphs*.) As is well known, a chief power of poetry is to foreshadow the future. In *Diderot's Harpsichord* Crevel had written, "All Poetry worthy of the name is a menace." A poet in the act of making poetry is a soul forever at the edge, on the brink. In the encounters between poets and the unborn whom they address, there is an overlap of two worlds, of the here-and-now with the elsewhere, the here-after. "Their death we live, and they ours," Heraclitus wrote of these moist souls that are always just about to be, but are never quite yet, reborn in the mind, invincibly wet behind the ears, of every fully conscious being.

In 1926, the year of *Difficult Death*, Madame Crevel died. Accord-ing to Klaus Mann (who says he was appalled), up to the very end the mere mention of her in front of René was apt to touch off fireworks. Jouhandeau, however, quotes a letter in which René says he is yearning for a day of mutual forgiveness but fears it will never come. Be that as it may, Madame Crevel served as the model of the hateful Madame Dumont-Dufour in *Difficult Death*, just as her son, the book's hero Pierre, was René himself. The same year, 1926, marked an encounter with psychoanalysis. Crevel soon abandoned therapy in disgust. He refused to believe in the Œdi-pus complex: "I was one of those who would have preferred to kill their Clytemnestra of a mother, rather than their Laius-like father." Before the Twenties were out, the youthful Jean-Paul Sartre was to dismiss Surrealism: "These turbulent young bour-geois want to wreck culture because it represents their Papa." With an appropriate transposition of parental gender, these words apply (although somewhat unfairly) to Crevel, who ap-pears to have been the only Surrealist who actually felt the sting of this kind of criticism.

INTRODUCTION

It may have been the last sensation he ever had. When those working-class guys from the factories showed up for his talk on Poetry and Art and Love and Revolution in June 1935, and after hearing him out, asked him questions he couldn't answer, something happened and René was blushing, then stammering, then reduced to speechlessness and left deeply humiliated. He had now to figure out for himself (like Pierre at the end of *Difficult Death*, stripped of everything and everyone, with no more hate, no more friendship, no more love) that to the insulted and the injured of this world who were getting it together at last to write their own script, he was just a rich kid with problems, slumming, or at this point a burned-out once-fashionable junkie in a world all his own, out of touch, spinning his wheels, completely and irretrievably full of shit, and it was the realization that this was the truth of the matter that burned to the very core of an at last absolutely honest man, true poet that he was, and killed him. Fifty years after the fact, it is clear that René Crevel wasn't the burn-out he thought himself in those last hours. What triumphs today is the inheritor of Rimbaud and Lautréamont and Orpheus making language sing with a freedom, an openness, a candor so total you want to drop everything and, just as he did, take it from there.

David Rattray
New York, 4/8/85

CREVEL
CHRONOLOGY

1900   Birth of René Crevel, second son of Eugène Paul Crevel, song publisher, in Paris: August 10

1914   Crevel's father commits suicide

1918   Crevel enrolls at the Sorbonne

1921   Meets Andé Breton and the Dadaists

1922   Initiates Breton in hypnotic techniques

1923   Appeared in Tristan Tzara's play *Le Cœur à gaz*, which was disrupted by Breton and his now anti-Dadaist friends

1924   Crevel joins Breton and the Surrealists; gets job as an editor at the magazine *Nouvelles littéraires*; first novel, *Detours*, published

1925   Hospitalized in a sanatorium with TB; for the rest of his life, Crevel spends part of each year in a hospital; intermittent alcoholism and drug addiction (opium, cocaine) from this point on; publication of second novel, *My Body and Me*

1926   Crevel's mother dies; third novel, *Difficult Death*

1927   Fourth novel, *Babylon*; joins French Communist Party

1928   Philosophical essay, *Mind Against Reason*

1929   Fifth novel, *Are You Crazy?*

1930   Essays in criticism: *Renée Sintenis, Paul Klee*

1931   Booklength essay, *Salvador Dalí, or, Anti-Obscurantism*

1932   Philosophical essay, *Diderot's Harpsichord*

1933   Sixth novel, *Putting My Foot In It*; expelled from CP

CREVEL CHRONOLOGY

1934   Crevel is readmitted to the CP

1935   Crevel attempts to conciliate Surrealists and Communist organizers of International Writers' Congress for the Defense of Culture; he commits suicide June 18

DIFFICULT DEATH

Chapter One

A BIT at a TIME

Mme. Dumont-Dufour and Mme. Blok are talking about an unpleasant topic: husbands. Mme. Dumont-Dufour (who would have been a judge like her father, the late Justice Dufour, had she but been born a man) denounces the law itself in a sweeping indictment of Society as a whole in terms that are not – you may take her word for it – minced:

"The law? The law is so stupid and prejudiced, it makes no difference my husband was raising hell for years, the option of divorce remains unavailable to me, his wife, even in this day and age."

Mme. Dumont-Dufour raises her eyes as if calling Heaven to witness (the ceiling will do in a pinch). Mme. Blok thinks her neighbor would not be out of her element in a grand salon adorned with fifty chandeliers, seventy-five Steinways, and an infinity of antique mirrors. Yet in truth no salon, however grand, could contain that of which Mme. Dumont-Dufour speaks. Her words conjure up a whole country, a continent, nay, much more: the domain of her memories. Domain of memories...A sunken city in the sea, which (my dear Mme. Blok) means deep water, because if Mme. Dumont-Dufour ever had any illusions they are long since at the bottom of the ocean. What's left, after all? Regrets, and memories of joyless acts. Who dares dream of the future? Were she one of those foolish women who indulge in daydreams, she could doubtless spend time dreaming up schemes of revenge. Mme. Dumont-Dufour loves pomp and ceremony; she never permits herself to be imposed upon save by the most exalted things, such as snow-capped mountains, or visiting cards black with titles, or plumed hearses, or wedding masses with their sparkling candlesticks, pollenless lilies, and families dressed to the nines. Mme. Dumont-Dufour prefers the majesty of ostrich plumes to the hue of birds of paradise. Alas, she is not only cheated of these high aspirations but must in addition refuse herself all hope of ever indulging her noble tastes. Were there such a thing as justice in this world, she, now in her sere and autumn time, would have done the honors of a domain of memories as calm and noble as La Maintenon's Versailles. Instead, being sufficiently self-assured in her pride to esteem the bracing virtues of humility and affirm, without waiting to be asked, that Man is dust and nothing else, yet ashamed of a second-rate past, she discovers the torture of having nothing to point to that might arouse envy in Mme. Blok. Her past, the domain of memories, is no better than any commonplace storeroom, one to which, however, she is not even allowed to relegate once and for all the paltry accessories of a former marriage, since, the fact remains, divorce is even now out of reach.

Does Mme. Blok know why?

Mme. Blok would only be too glad to know, but is afraid of appearing indiscreet. A sovereign wave of the hand dismisses all such qualms.

Do secrets come between them, then? Why? Both have suffered. Why, therefore, should their confidences spare those torturers, men? They are sisters, after all, sisters in misery.

"Sisters in misery…" The phrase is Mme. Dumont-Dufour's, needless to say, and she takes a justifiable pride in it, just as she prides herself on the Moroccan copper trays and China vases that adorn this drawing room in Paris's most elegant suburb, Auteuil. "Sisters in misery – plenty of mileage in that one," Mme. Dumont-Dufour tells herself.

A silence. The two women's motionless bodies have a hollow look about them. Mme. Dumont-Dufour's concept of the infinite derives from her idea of a vacuum, and it would not take much

DIFFICULT DEATH

prompting for her to imagine that her soul had been sucked up by one of those carpet-sweeping machines.

But now Mme. Blok's eyes are brimming with tears. If the truth be known, this wetness around the lids and these trembling nostrils are to be explained neither by the painful memories nor the tenderness offered along with tea and toast, nor yet by the panoramic spectacle of desolation evoked by Mme. Dumont-Dufour in her every turn of phrase. No, for once, the truth is perfectly simple: Mme. Blok hungers. She hungers to know.

Mme. Blok lives with her daughter, Diane. And Diane is all over the place at once – cinema, theater, friends' houses, God only knows where else – all those places where today's young girls venture without thinking twice – and Diane certainly knows more about it than her mother, seeing that she dances, attends teas and cocktail parties, paints, knows artists. Diane never speaks. She dispatches her meals in three mouthfuls. Her mouth opens only to eat.

Her poor mother thus knows nothing of a world from which she has been exiled by her misfortunes.

There is, of course, her cousin, Bricoulet. Honoré Bricoulet. He arrives at ten in the morning, kisses Mme. Blok on both cheeks, and intimates that widowers (it will soon be ten years since Mme. Bricoulet was torn from the affections of her dear Honoré) and widows (M. Blok committed suicide more than a decade ago) make good couples. Mme. Blok softens. Bricoulet inquires about her money affairs, then, each time, asks for more details concerning M. Blok's suicide, and decides to raise the siege only when Diane, who loathes the sight of him, comes in for lunch and by way of a salutation mocks him to his face.

When Bricoulet is gone, Mme. Blok summons up the courage to rebuke Diane.

"You weren't nice to Cousin Honoré."

"That dirty duck." (Bricoulet makes quacking sounds when he talks.)

"Diane, you're not being fair."

"I daresay he whispered more sweet nothings in your ear,

softened you up, proposed. Poor mother! He wants our piggy-bank. He's nothing but a gold digger. He'd skin a louse for the hide."

Diane sings: "Bricouli, bricoulouse, fleece a flea, flay a mouse..."
She concludes in a stage whisper: "Beware of Bricoulet."

"Diane, he makes you angry so you see it all wrong."

"Mother, you're not what interests him. He's interested in your misfortunes. The only thing he loves is misery. Your friend Honoré has got funny tastes. I've been told he adores lung, veal lung. He eats the same supper as his cat."

Diane could go on and on. Bricoulet inspires her. Mme. Blok is obliged to shut her up. The saddest part is that Cousin Honoré has become aware of Diane's hostility. His visits are already becoming rare. And Mme. Blok had wanted to ask him a few things about Mme. Dumont-Dufour and, especially, her invisible husband whom Honoré knew at school. She would also have liked to have had a man of experience give her an opinion on Mme. Dumont-Dufour's son, Pierre Dumont, a possible son-in-law, since he is Diane's best friend at art school.

But Bricoulet has avenged himself on the mother for her daughter's enmity, and until this very afternoon Mme. Blok has known nothing of Mme. Dumont-Dufour, whose neighbor she was last summer at the seaside. To be sure, August is not a month for confidences, so it took this autumn day in a drawing room in Auteuil – all gray and without a memory of white beach togs – for these two ladies to discover each other as...sisters in misery.

And so, because Mme. Blok is incautious enough to admit that she is bored more or less non-stop from January 1st on through to the following New Year's Eve, with Saturday Symphony matinées her sole distraction, Mme. Dumont-Dufour promises a series of hen parties, which brings tears to the eyes of her sister in misery, just as the thought of a good dish makes a gourmand's mouth water.

Quick to size up her audience, once having discovered this appetite, Mme. Dumont-Dufour has decided to hold back before serving up the feast. First, a few basic truths as hors d'œuvres.

DIFFICULT DEATH

Mme. Blok bites her lips as Mme. Dumont-Dufour rises above mere persons, facts, and things.

Nothing could oppose her ascension.

The word "compassion" falls in the middle of a sentence. Time for a brief dissertation.

Compassion this, compassion that, oh yes compassion my dear, compassion. And Mme. Dumont-Dufour declares that she has never neglected to make a habit of it. Besides, how could we live without it? There is no such thing as perfection in this world. Kindness costs very little. Also, one doesn't know where, on whom or on what, to lay the blame. So many factors are involved – chance, heredity, unhealthy tendencies. Poor Mme. Dumont-Dufour! In spite of a methodical mind, a rational intelligence, and a prudent heart, nothing has worked out for her. Thus Pierre, her son, whose nurse was an alcoholic (factor of chance), has an unstable character. Besides, he comes by it naturally – his father (factor of heredity) always had a vile temper. But all that would amount to nothing, if Pierre did not have bizarre tastes and curiosity to match (unhealthy tendencies) to the point that his mother is frantic, and with good reason. We may rejoice at his affection for our darling Diane. How can we not by the same token expect the worst, most catastrophic results from his friendship with foreigners who come from God only knows where? Yes, foreigners. France, Paris, and worst of all, Pierre Dumont, all are in their clutches. Young people have lost their heads. Mme. Blok should be careful with Diane. Mme. Dumont-Dufour has no choice but to let Pierre come and go at will, but she suffers enough for it, poor woman. All those sleepless nights and dark days. The flesh is weak. Twentieth-century youth are yielding to all the temptations of the modern Babylon and are concocting new ones with each passing year. In Mme. Blok and Mme. Dumont-Dufour's day, boys fell in love with the women at Maxim's, "birds," as M. Dumont used to say. Girls dreamed of gypsies with their dashing outfits and gorgeous mustaches. Nowadays the women of Maxim's are replaced by God only knows what adventuresses, prostitutes of every land and sex. There are no more gypsies, only saxophone-playing

Negroes. They have invented new vices, drinks, drugs – where will it all end? Mme. Dumont-Dufour is more than right to say that we must have compassion. She knows whereof she speaks, she knows little else. My God, what a painful experience it is, merely to exist in this day and age.

Too bad for Mme. Blok, who is dying of impatience in an Aubusson tapestry chair. Today Mme. Dumont-Dufour has the soul of a criminal judge, or a lawyer. Never has she felt more inspired. She lets go, in a display of rhetoric that would have done Justice Dufour, her father, proud, and he was never one to shrink from the grand manner, least of all in the home. Her voice glides over the theme of unhappiness with the majesty of a black swan. Is she to die amid these sticks of furniture that have witnessed all her tribulations in the presence of a visitor who cannot follow her in her flight? She pronounces her own eulogy, bearing down upon each syllable, prolonging it, repeating it, caressing it with her tongue as if it carried with it the promise of a forever-liberating sleep. True, for a time she did contemplate using her mastery of language to defend herself from Pierre's insolence and the world's malice. But now, in her despair, she has accepted Death, she calls for it and weaves these flowers of eloquence into funereal wreaths in which to drape herself, a statue of Unhappy Marriage. Mme. Blok is chafing at the bit. She would like to rise and ask Mme. Dumont-Dufour if she intends to waste her time with this rubbish all day long. Much more and the peace-loving Mme. Blok might consider an ultimatum. Tell me this minute why you can't get a divorce, or else…

Alas, unable to get a word in edgewise, Mme. Blok is informed that we mustn't be oversevere, a revelation that ought to lead somewhere. The long-awaited disclosure is coming! Mme. Blok hastens to agree:

"We mustn't be oversevere!"

"Obviously – but," pursues the tireless Mme. Dumont-Dufour, "there are limits." Take her husband, Dumont. Did he not indulge in such disgusting excesses that to disassociate herself from him – even on their honeymoon they were never close – she appended to the legally required married name (as if thereby proportionately to diminish it) the immeasurably more honorable name of her late father, Justice Dufour?

So it had come to pass that Mme. Edgar Dumont became Mme. Dumont-Dufour.

These twinlike patronyms dangling at either end of a hyphen are actually somewhat of a consolation to Mme. Dumont-Dufour. However, disliking easy successes, she is loath to betray her pride in the name Mme. Dumont-Dufour to Mme. Blok whom she suspects of being Jewish.

She is nevertheless unable to resist thinking out loud to the effect that compound names, despite their apparent simplicity, are a key to what the aristocracy might be in this century if anyone still cared to recognize the merits of the French middle-class which, my dear, has never ceased to provide an élite in the service of our country.

Mme. Dumont-Dufour, for instance, is the daughter of a jurist, the late Justice Dufour; and her husband – unworthy as he may otherwise be – is a military officer, Colonel Dumont.

Full stop.

Cousin Bricoulet has never told Mme. Blok that Dumont was a colonel. But colonel explains everything. Mme. Blok fills the drawing room with an "Ah!" exactly like that which Christopher Columbus cannot have failed to utter when he discovered America.

Mme. Dumont-Dufour quickly pulls the rug out from under Mme. Blok:

"Don't imagine it's because M. Dumont is a colonel that I am unable to divorce him and thus find myself condemned to a card without my own first name!"

Tracing the letters in the air onto an imaginary bristol card, M-A-D-A-M-E D-U-M-O-N-T – D-U-F-O-U-R, Mme. Dumont-Dufour wonders out loud if there was ever anything more wretched than a card without one's own first name.

How about the ocean without fish? is what Mme. Blok would like to say in reply. She can no longer help thinking that Mme. Dumont-Dufour is something of a *poseuse*.

Nevertheless, she labors to maintain an air of sympathetic resignation and shakes her head in agreement, first up and down, then from side to side. However, Mme. Dumont-Dufour, intent on sparing her new friend none of the details, adds:

"I'm not yet forty-four and no one ever calls me Louisa anymore. I was baptized Louisa by my poor stepmother who..."

After compassion, after the painful experience of existence, now the stepmother.

Mme. Blok is not going to take this lying down. She interrupts:

"Your stepmother did the right thing when she named you Louisa, you have nothing to complain about. Louisa Dufour is a lovely name. What a pity you can't get a divorce and make a new life.

"Make-a-new-life, make-a-new-life..."

What an air of reverie on this countenance of conjugal martyrdom! But Mme. Blok knows full well that the daughter of the late Justice Dufour is no dreamer; Mme. Blok swears to herself she won't let the wool be pulled over her eyes, but actually doesn't have time to complete the thought before she is asked:

"How about yourself, dear, what's your first name?"

Mme. Blok pronounces her given name, "Herminie." Time for compliments.

"Herminie, what a gentle name."

"Louisa's energetic."

"Herminie's innocent."

"Louisa's witty."

"Herminie's golden-haired." (Mme. Blok is a blonde.)

"Louisa...brunette..." (Mme. Dumont-Dufour's hair is as black as a crow.)

"Herminie...affectionate!"

"Louisa...Louisa..." (All right, Mme. Blok won't be a bitch.)

"Louisa's a name...worthy...of an empress."

"You really think Louisa's good?"

"Of course I do."

And, without transition, Mme. Blok returns to the charge:

"Louisa Dufour – what character! And what a pity you can't get a divorce."

DIFFICULT DEATH

"Yes, a great pity. But you can't know how happy I am that you like Louisa. My son Pierre never stops making fun of my name. He even goes so far (young people have lost all sense of respect) as to claim that Louisa is a typical call girl's name. The other day he had the gall to say that in front of your cousin, Bricoulet. I say he ought to be slapped, even if he did just turn twenty. And, I ask you, would my father have permitted me to be baptized with a... call girl's name?"

Mme. Blok's heels are digging into the carpet.

"You were telling me, my dear, that you couldn't get a divorce. Why not?"

The victim of the laws of men slowly collects herself:

"Because Colonel Dumont is..."

The tone of hushed confidence requires that her voice drop to a whisper at the end of the sentence. Mme. Blok fails to catch the last word. She shrieks,

"What?"

There being no more room for further stage effects, all stops are pulled out. In a triumphal tone:

"Colonel Dumont is mad, mad, mad..."

Only yesterday at Saturday Symphony they were doing Bach. Mme. Blok's ears are still ringing with the challenge, from *Phœbus and Pan*, "Mad, mad, mad, thy wits have gone astray," and now the madness of a Colonel in the army of the Third Republic turns it into a duet: "Mad, mad, mad..."

Mme. Dumont-Dufour, who has a respiratory problem, is the first to break off.

Mme. Blok follows suit. Once more, there is a pause. Mme. Blok takes advantage of it by picturing the Colonel in her mind's eye. The Colonel must have a mustache all the way round his face, in the style of 1907. The Colonel's mustache...Mme. Blok's virtuous aspirations are in vain, she must admit to herself that she finds her widowed state difficult. Diane is constantly advising her to remarry, but will hear nothing of Bricoulet though the latter is the only match possible. So Mme. Blok, who is afraid of her daughter, remains faithful to the memory of Dimitri Blok. It's all very well for Diane to talk, it's not easy for a widow to abstain. Thus, at the mere thought of the Colonel's mustache, poor Herminie is all hot and bothered. She has ants in her fingertips, feels up the arms of her chair, and tells herself the Colonel's mustache must tickle in a kiss. But who said anything about kissing, anyway? What would Diane think if she knew the kind of thoughts her mother was having? Diane, daughter, duty. But these once yielded precedence to Dimitri Blok, sex, and marriage. Yet now, since Bricoulet is at best a pig in a poke, basically there's nothing, nobody. Oh, if there were only a Colonel! In their heyday the Bloks had had a villa at La Baule. One of their neighbors, back from Madagascar with his naval commander's stripes and ravaging fevers, was in the habit of proclaiming in a loud, rough voice, "I'm fit as a fiddle." Fit as a fiddle. Mme. Blok likes fit, lean men, flat bellies like crucified Christs. "Fit as a fiddle" is how Colonel Dumont must be. A fiddle. Fiddle, fiddle, fiddle. Mme. Blok blushes; she has not forgotten the meaning in which the word was used by the heroine of a lewd revue to which M. Blok took her a few days after they got married. Your fiddle, sir. The word was used in such a precise sense...Mme. Blok turns bright pink. Fortunately, Mme. Dumont-Dufour is deeply absorbed in the contemplation of a tea-napkin. As for the Colonel (if there is a Colonel) he cannot fail to be thin. No doubt he was posted to Africa. Tropical heat caused softening of the brain. At least it prevented him from getting fat. And then he must have gone in for various sports. In any case, he rides. Therefore no potbelly. Exactly as she imagined. Fit as a...oooh, those naughty thoughts keep coming back. The Colonel's...thin, there! And then an officer, if he does start losing his trim figure, never need hesitate to don a corset. Colonel Dumont is a good-looking man; why on earth did he go mad?

Mme. Blok visualizes a strapping devil with red breeches, salt-and-pepper hair, dress tunic covered with gold braid, striding up and down from dawn to dusk in an institutional courtyard. His eyes are green in a deeply tanned, weatherbeaten face with no end of mustache. What a martial bearing! There's a man for you. He's a horse of a different color from that fair-haired son of his,

Pierre, that Diane is infatuated with. To be sure, Pierre also has green eyes, but the Colonel's are bigger and brighter because his face is all tanned. His eyes. The least thing can fill them with horror, and they react to each fleeting nightmare as the surface of a lake reflects the slightest passing cloud.

A madman.

But actually, is the Colonel all that mad, really and truly one-hundred percent mad?

"Is he mad?" Mme. Dumont-Dufour rejoins, "I think I know something about that. Didn't I tell you he doesn't even have the right to get a divorce? He's a basket case."

Then, taking the visitor's hands and calling her by her first name: "Herminie! Poor dear Herminie!"

"Louisa! Poor dear Louisa!" replies the echo of the Auteuil drawing room.

The two chairs are pulled closer together. A head bows to weep on a shoulder. At the same moment, a fur piece slides from the same friendly shoulder. A small, brittle crash. Bits of teacup on the floor, a fine China piece one had been made to admire before being allowed to use it. Mme. Blok cannot begin to excuse herself.

"No harm's done! For God's sake, Herminie, don't look so heart-broken. What does a teacup, even the most precious China one, matter to someone who has just found a friend...because you are my friend, aren't you, Herminie?"

"Oh yes, Louisa. I do understand. I have suffered, too. It's true I didn't have your good sense, your judgment, your sound instincts..." (Herminie's turn to wax eloquent). "I destroyed my life, I went ahead and married Dimitri Blok. I got carried away, he had such beautiful hands, I never suspected."

"You did make a mistake. But look here, one can do all the right things, and still suffer. I'm no nut, but that didn't prevent my husband from being a lunatic." As if an avenging deity were speaking through her mouth, Mme. Dumont-Dufour hammers it out: "A basket case, I told you and I repeat, a BASKET CASE. Ah, a Colonel he may have been, but gambling, drinking, and whoring have reduced him to a pretty state!"

RENE CREVEL

Mme. Blok tells Mme. Dumont-Dufour that having heard some stories from her cousin Bricoulet, who is friends with an asylum director somewhere in the Seine-Inférieure, she is not unaware of the strange turns madness can take. From a psychiatrist, Bricoulet has collected so many stories that at dinner parties he starts with the soup and continues until it is time to leave with stories whose main subject is the folklore of asylums. Hostesses need not wear themselves out over the direction in which table talk or drawing room conversation is going. Honoré holds the floor unchallenged and with such unerring brilliance that fellow guests may (according to individual temperaments) be in for hours of hilarity, anger, or consternation.

"But the cases M. Bricoulet tells of are mild alongside the Colonel."

"Mild? Bricoulet knows his case histories; he knows some pretty amazing ones, too."

"That may well be, but they would still not even come close to the Colonel. I mean – really, my dear, just imagine – for the past four years, every morning, the Colonel has written the same letter – oh, not to me, needless to say..."

And Mme. Dumont-Dufour, who could have made as good a Sphinx as a judge, propounds an enigma to Mme. Blok:

"Guess to whom, over the past four years, Colonel Edgar Dumont, colonel and madman, has been daily writing a letter in which the same words and all other details occur in exactly the same order, down to the last punctuation marks, commas, dots on the i's, accents, et cetera. Guess. I give you ten guesses. I give you a hundred, I give you ten thousand. Guess..."

Mme. Blok, being in no way inclined to lag behind the truth, begs off:

"I have no imagination."

Without further ado, Mme. Dumont-Dufour proclaims:

"Every morning Colonel Dumont writes to Madame de Pompadour."

"Madame de Pompadour?"

"In person."

DIFFICULT DEATH

"The mistress of Louis XV. How very odd."

"It's more than odd, it's extraordinary, and what is even more so is the fact that the letters are all perfectly identical and can be matched like prints from the same plate – a photograph of his subconscious, the doctor said."

Mme. Blok is lost in amazement.

Mme. Dumont-Dufour resumes, "Photographs of his subconscious mind. I'm none the prouder for them. A photograph of his subconscious – a lot of good that does us. They make me laugh with their scientific jargon, none of which can prevent my poor little Pierre from being the son and me the wife of a madman."

Sobs: "A madman."

The echo replies, "Madman…"

"Imagine, two months from now the Colonel will have completed fifteen hundred identical letters. He's already had a paper on him submitted to the Academy of Medicine. But the paper remains unpublished, so that's eyewash…"

Then, doing the honors of her husband's psychosis as she had just done those of her apartment:

"Would you like to see one of the letters? As you can imagine, the asylum doesn't keep all of them. If the Colonel lived another twenty years, an annex would have to be added, just to preserve the fruits of his industry. The doctor gave me several; I have them in my desk; I'll get them for you…"

Mme. Dumont-Dufour returns with two of the letters. "Look, compare. As you can see, this comma on the third line corresponds exactly to the comma on the third line of the other. Look, compare."

Lifting her lorgnette, Mme. Blok looks, compares, and reads:

*To Madame de Pompadour
despite Time & Space*

Madame,

I salute you.

Make no mistake about it – coming from the sunken-eyed tenement of clay in which perforce I dwell, the present letter is no mere casual greeting.

RENE CREVEL

Madame, I am a prisoner in Ratapoilopolis.

The persecution began already at Saint-Cyr, where fellow cadets nicknamed me "Ratapoil."* It continues to this day, and — although a colonel and an inventor — I am condemned to rot in a rambling edifice, in (I repeat, Madame) this sunken-eyed tenement of clay in which perforce I dwell. Rest assured, Madame, that no colonel having served under the colors of the Third Republic could write to you without being perfectly aware of the unfavorable sort of construction that might be put on such a correspondence. Colonel Dumont is writing to...La Pompadour! I can just see the looks on their faces — the Freemasons, my wife, the Minister of War, the Admiralty, and every officer in the entire French navy.

All will maintain that I am a lunatic, as they have in fact constantly done ever since Algeria, where one day I discovered the means of eliminating the need for gunboats, by attaching fins fashioned of palm leaves to the wheels of cannon. Each field piece was thus readily convertible at no extra cost into a "fish-cannoneer." The Fish-Cannoneer...Because my invention displeased the Minister of War, the Admiralty, and the officers (all of whom it rendered obsolete), in league with my wife they locked me up in Ratapoilopolis with the insane. And here, amid mental and sentimental monstrosities, I remain, alone in the possession of my faculties and of my inventive genius.

Madame, an old soldier like myself is not much of a hand at letter-writing, so I'll not beat about the bush. I supplicate you in the goodness of your heart because, quite frankly, you are not what is commonly known as a good wife. Brava! I've had my fill of them. Madame Dumont is such a wife, and it is my impression that at close quarters and at a distance she is a simple pain in the arse.

A pain in the arse...Pardon the expression, Marquise. It is crude, I admit, but it alone conveys some idea of the character and nature of the person in question, for if I am not yet quite insane, this does not mean that Justice Dufour's fair daughter, my spouse, has ever left undone anything that might conduce thereto. In the most innocent of pleasures she could uncover a crime: "What's the meaning of vermouth at the dinner hour? If you persist, I shall hide this bottle as I already did the cognac bottle. You were seen coming out of a disreputable establishment. Have you no shame? A colonel in the Army of the Third Republic, indeed! Noblesse oblige!" And she went on like that all day long.

Madame Dumont has (parenthetically) changed her name to Madame Dumont-

*Translator's note: Ratapoil (literally, "naked rat") was a cartoon character by Daumier, synonymous with "agent provocateur, goon."

DIFFICULT DEATH

Dufour, as though ashamed to bear the name of one of the 20th century's greatest inventors. But she is not the only one I have no choice but to regard as an enemy. I have no fewer grievances against the government of this Republic.

So much the worse if the present letter falls into the hands of my wife, the Minister of War, the Admiralty, or the Freemasons. I say that the Republic, with her stone body, her steely bust and maid of all work's apron, is a monster that walks barefoot in plowed fields.

And indeed, Madame, she could never learn to wear those pretty shoes whose heels were the glory of your royal master's reign, those Louis Quinze heels in which no good wives of the Madame Dumont-Dufour type could ever walk. From Ratapoilopolis, Madame, I supplicate you and your high heels. Remaining your most humble & obdt. svt., Madame,

Colonel DUMONT

Mme. Dumont-Dufour asks, "What do you say to that?"

Mme. Blok makes a gesture indicating that her silence does not proceed from an absence of thoughts on the subject.

Mme. Dumont-Dufour resumes on an indulgent note:

"Poor Colonel Dumont, he is more to be pitied than blamed. Yes, every time Pierre comes home in the middle of the night, or a bit the worse for wear, don't you know, I point out his father's example to him...as one not to be imitated. Pierre has seen where drink and dissipations lead. Today's young people are strange, Madame Blok. Pierre could never get along with his father while the Colonel was still living at home. Well, would you believe it, now he sides with him on any and all occasions. At times his judgment of people and things is so peculiar that I find myself wondering whether he, too, might not be destined to end up in 'Ratapoilopolis.'

" 'Ratapoilopolis' – what a name! He had to have been out of his mind to make up such a thing, the Colonel especially – in his normal state he never had any imagination. Polis means city in Greek, you know. Ratapoilopolis, city of Ratapoils. At Saint-Cyr they called the Colonel Ratapoil because he was exceptionally hairy."

Mme. Blok starts thinking about the Colonel's hair. Hair on his

17

torso, arms, legs, all over. She closes her eyes. M. Blok's body was white, smooth, hairless. Mme. Blok has ants in her fingertips again, at the thought of how much she enjoyed running her hands over that perfect skin.

All the same, hairless skin can be a bore. The Colonel's body hair...a broad chest densely overgrown with hair like a rugged prairie, narrowing down to a point between slender hips. Mme. Blok closes her eyes. How hard it is to endure the widowed state. It's a good thing Bricoulet is no Lothario, because poor Herminie's Indian summer is so warm she would end up giving in. Strange that at this very moment she should recall that Dimitri, who was by no means shy in bed, used to call her "my dear little chippie." Mme. Blok is no foolish virgin, and yet what a state it puts her in, merely to think of a man — a Colonel. She pictures her dainty, plump gloved hand, now at rest on the arm of her chair, groping the Colonel's pectoral fleece. Blok used perfume. The Colonel must smell a lot better than Oeillet or Fougère de Saint-Germain. Any wide-open pair of nostrils pointed his way must get a whiff of Africa — lion, wild beast, real man, uh-huh!

Mme. Blok, no longer bashful, asks, "He must have gotten quite thin out there in Ratapoilopolis?"

"Yes, and God knows he was already fit — as fit..."

"...as a fiddle," Mme. Blok interjects breathlessly.

"That's it — fit as a fiddle...and brutal."

"My husband was so gentle, it seemed almost a bit unhealthy toward the end. In the Colonel you must at least have a remembrance of someone...male."

"A male? Am I then such a female that the remembrance, as you put it, of a male would be so agreeable to me as you seem to imagine? Those things have never interested me, Madame."

Then, to rub it in, she proceeds to explain:

"Love, Madame Blok, physical love, that is, the kind of love that only men of my husband's type and women interested by that type are capable of — love is a pretty disgusting business. For one thing, it stains the sheets unless one is careful. For another, it smells nasty."

DIFFICULT DEATH

Mme. Blok interrupts: "It smells nasty – how can you say that? I don't know anything about art and even less about literature, Madame, but I love music and am mad about perfumes. Well, if you had a nose for it, you'd know that all odors basically, if you smell them closely and carefully, smell like...yes, perfection."

"Well," Mme. Dumont-Dufour shoots back, "the Colonel just smelled like a billygoat. The hair on his legs pricked me. And so, after our son was born, we moved into separate rooms. Besides, even during our honeymoon, the Colonel never gave up frequenting houses of ill-fame. I was not so hungry for affection I had to content myself with what sluts and strumpets had left over."

"I, on the contrary," says Mme. Blok, "bestowed forgiveness on my Dimitri every night, and even, in the early days of our marriage, if he happened to take it into his head..." (Mme. Blok is embarrassed) "yes, if he took it into his head, even afternoons..."

"Afternoons! You were a weak woman, Herminie!"

"I needed love, Louisa."

"And 'love' is what you call the exactions of a man in rut? All those dirty acts. It makes me feel dirty just to think of them, and I'm no prude, either. Can kisses be that disturbing, Herminie?"

"I always felt warm against Dimitri's breast. All he had to do was put his arm around my waist and I felt good."

"Admit it – Dimitri Blok got under your skin."

"I'll be glad to admit it, if you like."

"So – a man got under your skin. You were in love. Poor dear. It never happened to me. Which is where I get my strength."

"I admire you, Louisa. I envy you."

"My father, Justice Dufour, brought me up to be a good wife, and a good wife I have remained."

"But," Mme. Blok confesses, "when I was only ten years old, I was already wondering what love might have in store. I'd sit for hours at a time, in the corner, without moving a muscle. My parents praised me for being such a good little girl; I was a bit ashamed of their compliments."

"You certainly ought to have been ashamed. I would have thrown you in a cold shower, if I'd been your mother."

19

"She had no idea what I was thinking."

"I should hope not."

Mme. Blok resumes the story of her life:

"Now I'm middle-aged, a widow. I have a grown daughter. My cousin, Bricoulet, would gladly marry me, but Diane hates him. I've been condemned to loneliness ever since the day Dimitri left me. I loved him, yet of his own choice he left me. He committed suicide."

"Good God! Business troubles?"

"No."

"An illegitimate child, perhaps?"

"Not that I know of."

"Might he by any chance have contracted some unmentionable disease? After all, one doesn't just kill oneself for no reason, my dear."

"Nevertheless, Dimitri had no business troubles, no illegitimate children, and no diseases."

"Well then?"

"He just killed himself."

"If he killed himself, there must be an explanation."

Mme. Dumont-Dufour's tone grows inquisitorial; she thinks the truth is being withheld. Mme. Dumont-Dufour has a clear head on her shoulders. Were she to be broken on the wheel, she would repeat until the end of time that, if Blok killed himself there was a reason and it was no idle one. Otherwise, he couldn't have died.

This line of reasoning leads Mme. Dumont-Dufour to cast doubt on the very fact of Blok's death. His own widow, Mme. Blok, protests; but her causalist friend's objections are so powerful that if the door flew open and Dimitri, suddenly restored to the living, strolled into the room, Herminie would not be altogether surprised.

"Are you saying, Louisa, that M. Blok isn't dead, that he never committed suicide?"

"If he is dead, if he did commit suicide, give me the reasons."

"Reasons, reasons?" Mme. Blok is not without reasons, yet none

DIFFICULT DEATH

that she cites is good enough to satisfy Mme. Dumont-Dufour.
And so she is frightfully sorry she can think of no others.

Mme. Dumont-Dufour insists, "Go on."

"All right, I will. First," Mme. Blok begins, intimidated, as if she
were taking her baccalaureate examination and unsure of herself
as if she had, for example, to name the western tributaries of the
Mississippi. "First, suicide runs in the Blok family. I was warned
of this before I married Dimitri, and my grandmother on rue de
Grenelle-Saint-Germain, who had married a redhead, and half of
the children favored their father and were red-haired, too – she
said to me, 'You know, little one, suicide is like carrot-heads,
purely a matter of chance. Some escape it, others don't.'"

"The Semitic background, no doubt..." Mme. Dumont-Dufour
insinuates.

"But, my dear, Dimitri wasn't Jewish. He was a Russian."

"Jew or Russian, I'm not sure which is worse. For God's sake,
Herminie, how could you have let yourself go to the extent of doing such a rash, irresponsible thing? Marry a Russian!"

"Dimitri was naturalized."

"Did that automatically change the blood in his veins?"

"Obviously not."

"So – you were a victim of Slavic charm, Herminie."

"I confess I was, Louisa."

"Are you sorry?"

Sitting erect in her armchair, Mme. Dumont-Dufour has the
mien of majesty. She resembles that Queen of England, Empress
of India, whose shoulder blades never had the weakness to touch
the back of a chair. Mme. Dumont-Dufour has the mien of majesty,
its stony features. She personifies Justice. Well might she be styled
"Grand Inquisitor" – to the superlative degree! Will she burn
Mme. Blok in her salamander, if the latter does not immediately
confess that she was indeed a victim of Slavic charm and thereupon abjure her error? Mme. Blok is starting to get nervous.
Mme. Dumont-Dufour bears down:

"Are you defending yourself?"

"There's such a thing as fate."

21

"Fate is just a word."

"Even though you were lucky enough not to fall in love, you yourself admit you've never been happy."

"Yes, but I have a clear head on my shoulders."

"And I a few happy memories. The night I got engaged, my wedding day, my wedding night."

"The night I got engaged, my wedding day, my wedding night," Mme. Dumont-Dufour crows. Really! With Mme. Blok, what is there to say? A wedding night...Mme. Dumont-Dufour bursts out laughing. She laughs herself purple, she laughs in her throat, nose, mouth, and eyes; laughter stretches wrinkles in her face and convulses her entire body, the bones of which seem to be coming apart at the joints inside her black Moroccan silk dress. When Mme. Dumont-Dufour laughs, she really laughs. A wedding night! Mme. Blok, this isn't possible, you're joking...a wedding night!

But Mme. Dumont-Dufour had not forgotten her wedding night.

In dress uniform, having insisted on an officer's ceremony, Dumont, whose rank was then captain, without even taking the time to pull off his boots, started biting her shoulder. He did not kiss her, no, he bit her on the right shoulder, near the collarbone – this while the new bride was attempting to disrobe in the couple's joint dressing room. Dumont's lips were like sandpaper, mustache like horsehair, and manner brutal. Then Mme. Dumont, who had in one minute made up her mind she was going to be a good albeit unhappy wife, closed her eyes and let herself be dragged to the bed where she allowed the Captain, who had still not taken off his boots, to become her husband. It all happened on top of the quilt she had embroidered with her own hands during their engagement – Dumont, sloppy as he was brutal, had even neglected to turn down the sheets. (And the victim of this bestial lust had endured it without ever asking herself whether the very pain that arose from it could one day give rise to the keenest pleasure.) Sated, the Captain let her drop, half-dead and covered with black-and-blue marks, in order to go and kick off his boots, breeches, and shirt; so when the young bride finally opened her eyes once more she found herself confronted by a strapping

DIFFICULT DEATH

body dressed only in its hair. Her gaze focused on certain details in red which rapidly increased in size to where a naked devil, of which the tender newlywed was horror-struck, inspired in her a sudden vision of a giant coffeepot in human form.

Such was the wedding night of Captain Dumont's bride. But since Mme. Blok has known ecstasies which her poor friend admits herself quite incapable of imagining, what in the name of God is Mme. Blok complaining about? And, since she claims her husband committed suicide, let her give us some reasons that will lend plausibility to his death.

It is argued, first, that suicide is a frequent thing in the Blok family. Secondly, a sensation-seeking husband who was always looking for something new may have killed himself merely in order to experience the sensation of death.

"Why, yes, that does make sense," Mme. Dumont-Dufour muses. "He was a Russian."

"God knows he was that. He was a typical Russian mystic, too! You should have heard the way he would carry on after a few drinks."

He would weep and squeeze Herminie tight in his arms. Then, in a hoarse voice, he would croak:

"Listen, woman. Earthly happiness is not enough for me. You and the little one are mere trivia. Dimitri Ossipovitch can never put limitations on his destiny."

Mme. Blok did her best to make him listen to reason.

"Trivia! Dimitri, you don't know what you're saying."

Then he would always hark back to his obsession: The Volga boatmen's hands are bleeding, the tow ropes are imprinted with the pain in their fingers; hunger has sculptured their faces. They are cold – or hot – who cares? Their songs, monotonous as the sky, sad as the river, taste as sweet to their hearts as a deep breath of one's own native air. "When will I see my native land again, when will I hear the Volga boatmen again, Herminie?"

"If you like singing, we'll go tomorrow to the Opéra-Comique. They're doing Le Roi d'Ys."

"Poor little girl, I'm not talking about any Roi d'Ys, or even any

23

song, I'm talking about a thing that is in the wind when it crosses our steppes and follows our rivers – and this thing may be found anywhere in Europe where the émigrés, exiles, and refugees from Siberia remember their motherland, Holy Russia."

"Holy Russia...I understand, Dimitri, but here in France you have your wife, your little Diane who will grow up, get married someday, and have children of her own."

"Who cares? The Volga boatmen, Herminie, what a sad lot, the monotony of their lives finally becomes a kind of happiness..."

After some minutes of silent reverie, he would persist: "My wife, my daughter – trivia. Diane will get married, have children. Good for her. I will still die for Russia, and I will not need any of your dirges and filthy words of commiseration. I forbid you to pray over my corpse. Take my carcass, dress it decently, and dig it a grave. I refuse to bequeath my body to the soil of Europe – bury me on the banks of the Volga in my own country! There let me turn into a fish and then one day let some fisherman take me home to his cabin, for the miracle of a resurrection on the shores of Russia, the Holy Russia out of which my poor father was hounded. Because I am an exile's son, and the Orthodox Church..."

Thereby hung a tangled tale involving the Czar and the Orthodox Church – of which Mme. Blok freely admits she understood not a jot. Blok then invariably concluded:

"Already my father, my grandfather killed themselves in order to escape the most wretched of all fates. I see their souls in the air around me. Greetings, Father, Ossip Alexandrovitch. Hello, Grandfather Alexander Fedorovitch! Soon Dimitri Ossipovitch will join you. Here on earth I have a wife, Herminie, and a daughter, Diane. Who cares? Besides, Herminie, you are only a European."

"Well, then, what are you?"

"A Russian, Herminie. A Russian, who despises this approximation of real life on which his strength is being squandered. I am sorry for you and little Diane who will get married someday and have children. I pity you, but pity will not fetter either my mind or my heart. Another shot of vodka!"

DIFFICULT DEATH

"Dimitri, aren't you drinking a bit too much?"

"What if I killed you with me, you and little Diane?"

"Dimitri, in the name of Heaven!"

"All right, I'll let you live."

At this point, more often than not, he went to sleep.

Mme. Dumont-Dufour protests. This fellow Blok treated his wife like the lowest of the low. Herminie was only a European! What was he, other than a savage, a Russian? To be sure, a Russian is a different story than a Jew, but in point of fact Mme. Dumont-Dufour would be hard put to say which was the better of the two. Russians, Jews, and then that postwar invention, Americans – precious little to be said for any of them. Pierre's best friend is an American. Mme. Dumont-Dufour has already told Mme. Blok about this Arthur Bruggle, who worked his way over to Europe as a dishwasher. Naturally, Pierre – who has a taste for the bizarre – marvels at Bruggle's sea voyage quite as much as he does at his father's insanity. Arthur Bruggle is a youth with long hands, the gait of a dancer, a panther's tread, and animal eyes. Quite a phenomenon. First, with a name like "Bruggle," he ought to have been pink-cheeked, cheerful, and clean-cut, in which case Pierre, who prides himself on being friends with the most spectacular freaks, would never have had anything to do with him. But let's drop Bruggle, the Americans, and the Jews, and get back to our Russians and M. Blok, toward whom his wife truly showed far too much indulgence. Why did she allow him to treat her so badly? It's not to be believed. What on earth did she expect from such a man?

"Nothing, Louisa..."

Nothing...Love alone bound their two destinies, the Slav's and Herminie's, together.

Of course. Love. Well, a sin admitted is half-remitted, and since Mme. Blok has confessed, let her not feel crushed with remorse – let her tell on. What about this suicide?

This suicide, in the mind of the woman who was bereaved by it, remains, in all of its details, yes, every last one of them, as fresh in her memory as if it had happened yesterday.

25

RENE CREVEL

Mme. Dumont-Dufour braces herself in her chair and utters a "Well then," the exact meaning of which is "Get on with it!"

And get on with it we do. Mme. Blok is already launched on her tale.

Early July, 1914. A Saturday evening. The Bloks are about to leave Paris, and Monsieur Blok's tailor has just delivered a new, broad-checked suit. Even here in Mme. Dumont-Dufour's drawing room eleven years later, poor Herminie can still see it all. Dimitri in shirtsleeves and shorts, romping with Diane. Remarkably lithe for his forty-odd years, he can do a neat (and dangerous) little somersault without the slightest effort. On the night of his death, to be sure, he had to content himself with a few *entrechats* because the Bloks were having people to dinner; thus, at a quarter after seven Madame interrupted her mate's fun so he could go get dressed.

Still in a perfectly good mood, joking, even – so he was, really and truly – he rings the maid, asks her to fix his shirt, etc....and just as he is putting on the shirt, Herminie – from the next room where she is exchanging her afternoon skirt and blouse for a brand-new evening gown, a little marvel in cream and pink satin – calls to Dimitri, "Darling, did you put the liquor out yet?"

"I forgot, dear. I'll go right now."

With that, he went into his study, where the liquor was kept.

Eight o'clock. Mme. Blok sits amid her guests, resplendent in cream and pink satin.

Eight-thirty. The guests exchange looks, conversation lags. A hand smooths out a wrinkle in the cream and pink satin.

A quarter to nine. The butler will advise Monsieur that dinner awaits his arrival to be served.

Ten of nine. The butler returns empty-handed. Monsieur is nowhere to be found, neither in his bedroom nor in his dressing room.

Five of nine. Mme. Blok can no longer open her mouth. But she imagines a volcano is about to erupt from each of her fingertips. She fidgets and would like to smash an insolent clock, an Empire clock she is coming to loathe, although only a few minutes ago she was still so proud of it.

Four minutes to nine. Three minutes to nine.

She gets up.

Two minutes to nine. She is standing in the midst of her guests, so pale in her cream and pink satin that the whole drawing room cries out as one man: "Herminie!" But not one of them stands up. Picture them – the Bloks' dinner guests, all glued to their chairs. The clock sounds one till. Which has gone crazy, Herminie or the clock? Neither one nor the other; but already the guests are no longer hungry. They know another feast has been promised. When all in a chorus, they shouted Mme. Blok's name it was not to beg her not to take another step forward, but to the contrary, to exhort her to do just that. It begins to dawn on Mme. Blok that a certain fatality is about to make her a sister of the most terrible gods. Sparks are flying in her mind, and out of the sparks a conflagration. Herminie's brain is on fire. A fire which lights up the circle of guests. The sallow, pale-eyed, black-lipped guests, death's heads, Death. Mme. Blok divines death. And a clock which no longer moves.

Nine o'clock at last. Exactly one hour since they should have announced, "Dinner is served." At this point witness Mme. Blok remembering that suicide runs in the Blok family, and Mme. Blok looking like stone inside her cream and pink satin, and Mme. Blok with her right hand on the knob of the door leading from the drawing room into the study, and Mme. Blok, a statue of woe, awaiting the last stroke of nine to open the door and make the announcement herself:

"Dimitri is dead."

Dimitri is dead...

...And the ferocity of the guests, whose looks hurl inexorable volleys of question marks.

Dimitri is dead. The mistress of the house had better explain: "Dimitri is dead, he committed suicide, he hanged himself."

The guests leap from their seats, rush to the door. The women make a perfunctory show of putting their bare arms in front of their eyes although all without exception are bound and determined not to miss the slightest gory detail. A hanged man. Imagine! And no one is listening, as Herminie laments: "Why did I ask him to get the liquor? He drank almost a whole bottle of vodka, then killed himself." She screams: "Dimitri, Dimitri!" The servants arrive, mingle with the guests. The chef (engaged for the evening from Rebattet's) dominates the situation in his white bonnet.

One of the men proposes to cut the body down. The women clap their hands. Mme. Blok, staggering against a wall, sees the guests hovering over Dimitri, whom they have laid out on a sofa. When they have gone through the motions of attempting to revive him, they excuse themselves and leave. Not without first having divvied up the rope. Brings good luck, you see. And when the *commissaire de police* arrives, his men will not find the least thread of it left.

Poor Herminie. Nonetheless, she is told that on the whole she was lucky, for supposing Blok had not died, what with his character and his immoderate taste for vodka, who knows, considering the stormwind of destruction and fury that has raged over the world in the intervening years, he might have quite simply gone Bolshevik.

Can the peace-loving Herminie, Diane's mother, picture herself with a Bolshevik husband? No, no, you're far better off with a suicide in the family, a suicide or even a madman – either is better than a Communist. The hammer and sickle? God Almighty! And Blok would probably have called the concierge "comrade."

It would have been better if her husband had chosen to depart this life on a day when there was no company. Moreover, had he been well-bred, he would never have hanged himself in his shirtsleeves. Yes, dying at one's own dinner party is in poor taste. It does M. Blok greater discredit than one can easily say. It more than hints at what such a man would have been capable of in later life. It also suggests his widow has plenty of spare time, if she can spare any to mourn him.

Summer of 1914, you say? If he was so determined to kill himself, why didn't he just wait a few weeks? What with the War, he could have had an honorable death. His wife and daughter, instead of being humiliated, could have been proud of him. Because (isn't it so, Herminie?) the War did at least have the advantage of rearranging quite a few things for many a family. If Mme. Dumont-Dufour had been born under a lucky star, there can be no doubt that Dumont would have died leading the troops into battle. Then he would have been a hero. There might even have been a street named after him in Auteuil. Instead of which, today in his padded cell he is good for nothing but to waste doctors' time and drive his own son crazy.

As for Dimitri Blok – since he is dead, long live Dimitri Blok! But since the ladies have sworn to tell all ("between sisters"), would Herminie – in view of the fact she has had a hanged man in her home – be so kind as to tell dear Louisa if what they say is true.

Herminie, terrified: "What do they say, Louisa?"

Louisa smiles. Feigning embarrassment, she lowers her voice to a confidential tone and, after some hemming and hawing, declares she is not going to beat about the bush, but if a mandragora did not sprout from the floorboards of the room where Dimitri hanged himself, she would nevertheless like to be clear and know whether there's any truth in what they say about hanged men, which she herself read in a novel whose title she no longer recalls but which she bought in a railroad station in order to pass away the time on board the train...

Mme. Blok does not understand.

What is Mme. Dumont-Dufour driving at?

The armchairs hitch closer together. Whispers. A delicate question. Mme. Blok gasps and blushes bright pink:

"I didn't look. It was the butler who undressed him and put him in his shroud. All I can tell you is that that broad-checked suit (which had never been worn) was immediately afterwards eaten up by moths in exactly that place – under the fly."

"Is that so?"

Mme. Dumont-Dufour will check with her doctor on this and inform her friend what he says.

Mme. Blok has the feeling she has done her duty; she has told enough stories; she may now get up and take her leave.

"But Herminie, dear, you only just arrived, we've hardly had a chance to talk; I didn't even get around to asking – how is your darling Diane?"

"Diane is marvelous. And Pierre?"

"Oh, Pierre is foolish as usual." Mme. Dumont-Dufour does not suffer from an overabundance of modesty – as she has already proved with the Ratapoilopolis story and the question about mandragora. Nonetheless, Mme. Dumont-Dufour would not venture to tell a quarter of the absurdities – no, the word is not strong enough – the improprieties – still too weak – one would almost have to say, the monstrosities that Pierre unhesitatingly commits. As she tells Pierre himself, Colonel Dumont – who, Lord knows committed many follies in his day – never even dreamed of some of the things Dumont junior is doing as a matter of course. Thus, for example, as if the day were not enough for him, he often gets up in the middle of the night. Colonel Dumont deceived his wife from five to seven, came home for dinner, and at nine-thirty was ready to (as he put it) hit the sack. Now that may have lacked propriety, but it at least had the merit of being more or less bearable. But Pierre, Pierre…

Mme. Blok gazes at the Moroccan coat rack which Mme. Dumont-Dufour, who has original ideas when it comes to furniture, has had constructed. Yes, "constructed" is the word – it's a real piece of architecture, with copper trays the Colonel brought back from Fez, and wood inlaid with mother-of-pearl, decorated with those Arabic characters that make such a pleasant effect. Copper trays, inlaid wood, it was all artistically blended and pieced together – add three hat-pegs and you have the piece which at the very entrance announces to visitors that they are entering the abode of a woman of taste. Well, last week this little marvel of Islamic artistry and European whimsy was nearly smashed by young Pierre Dumont:

"I had at last managed to get to sleep, when at 3 A.M. I woke up with a start. There was a terrible rumpus out here. I thought it was burglars. Well, I get up, take my fire tongs to defend myself, and rush to the front hall. The coat rack was overturned on the floor and underneath the coat rack, my dear, was none other than my son, thrashing about, hat still on but cockeyed, collar undone, glassy-eyed, hands trembling, in such a condition that I wouldn't have touched him even with the tongs.

"I imagine you think Pierre was embarrassed? Not in the least. To the contrary, he seemed wholeheartedly amused and laughed at my curlers and nightgown. No doubt the ladies he frequents are in the habit of sleeping stark naked. The proprieties to him are all ridiculous. I can still hear him hiccuping, 'Nighties, night (hic!) gowns…' I tried to help him to his feet. I said, 'Pierre, you've been drinking! You're not drunk, you're absolutely smashed, and you had better take another look at the example set by your father in his padded cell.'

"But try to reason with that young maniac. He caught me by the hem of my nightgown and pulled so hard he ripped it. He kept saying he was going to tell me all his secrets, every one of them. Then he turned around and said, 'I want to have some more fun. Maman, put on your hat and let's go to Montmartre for some whiskey!'

"That was the last straw. I went back to my room and spent the rest of the night crying my heart out. I was hoping for an apology in the morning. Well, the minute he woke up, he was on the telephone – come to think of it, he was speaking with your daughter, Diane, telling the whole thing, my curlers, my nightie as he calls it, while at the same time praising his foreign friends and that whole crowd that are turning our young people's heads and setting our families on their ears. And all I wanted out of life was to see my grandchildren come into the world."

"But your son could marry."

"I shouldn't be too sure of that, if I were you, considering his most recently acquired tastes…" Mme. Dumont-Dufour would appear to be implying quite a lot. Mme. Blok is no ignoramus. She knows love is a many-headed Hydra.

Mme. Blok is a mother, too. It is all very well to give Diane her

RENE CREVEL

head, but Mme. Blok's duty is to leave no stone unturned, to know exactly what to expect from her daughter's friends.

Gently, but firmly, she asks:

"Would Pierre be abnormal, by any chance?"

Mme. Dumont-Dufour reserves to herself the rights of a government ministry, and she does not like her people to be accused (except of course for the Colonel who is no longer an accredited member of the family). She alone can judge, condemn, absolve.

Thus, when Mme. Blok repeats her question, "Is Pierre abnormal?" Mme. Dumont-Dufour shrugs good-naturedly:

"No, he's simply a bit degenerate."

"Degenerate!" growls a voice behind the door.

"Speak of the devil," says Mme. Dumont-Dufour, "here comes our Pierre."

Pierre is already in the room.

"Hello, Madame Blok. Hello, mother of a degenerate."

"Hello, Pierre."

"Hello, son."

"Are you abnormal, Madame Blok?"

"Pierre, please."

"Are you degenerate, Mother?"

"What ails you, Pierre?"

Mme. Blok thinks she had better leave. She gets up. Good-bye. Good-bye. Say hello to Diane. Let's get together again soon, dear. Mme. Dumont-Dufour and her son are left alone.

Chapter Two

RATAPOILOPOLIS?

Pierre ambles around the table, on which the urn and tea-things are still present, the sugar bowl, tea-cloth, cups, saucers, and everything else used for tea by a gentlewoman who loves order and a certain reasonable modicum of luxury.

Pierre selects a small square of diaphanous linen and in the twinkling of an eye rips it to shreds. Of a pæan to the loom there remains nothing but a few shreds strewn underfoot. "That's better!" the young vandal snarls, and then, looking his mother straight in the eye: "You make me laugh."

The Auteuil drawing-room is a Calvary where an unhappy woman awaits fresh tortures while the boy, a caged lion if there ever was one, makes mincemeat of anything she says. The unhappy woman bends over (Lord, what a vicious world, the poor thing's joints creak like a skeleton!) to pick up the shreds one by one from the carpet and then, as Pierre whistles to himself – goodness, he thinks he's in a stable – stands up red-faced to ask:

"Have you lost all sense of respect?"

"Sense of respect?"

Mme. Dumont-Dufour takes a fresh "You make me laugh!" full in the face and is treated to the spectacle of Pierre holding his sides as if he were going to die laughing. Mme. Dumont-Dufour has not said her last word; even now she seeks (give us this day our daily bread) the right opener for a scene she neither can nor should miss.

No use beating about the bush.

Flatly:

RENE CREVEL

"Pierre, I am waiting for an explanation."

"What explanation?"

"You know as well as I do."

Pierre does not know, and remarks that if an explanation were called for, it would take until the middle of next week; but, for starters, would Mme. Dumont-Dufour, before she begins ranting and raving, kindly tell her son why she called him a degenerate?

That tears it. So Pierre has got the audacity to ask why his mother called him a degenerate, as if he didn't know of all the evidence supporting that verdict.

To begin with, Pierre's friends. Mme. Dumont-Dufour, ever a repository of wit and wisdom, fires off a quick "Show me the company, I'll show thee the man" and then enumerates the unwholesome tendencies and vices (which she admits she lacks the innate perversity to imagine in all their details) indulged in by these artists from God knows where in America who come to Europe as dishwashers.

"You mean Bruggle," Pierre interrupts. "If he washed dishes on a steamer..."

"A-hah, I see what you're leading up to. You can't even put your own life in order and at the same time see no one worthy of imitation besides these foreign tramps and drifters that are on the point of taking this country over."

Pierre shrugs his shoulders.

Mme. Dumont-Dufour resumes:

"And your friends aren't all that's wrong with you. To confront you with the whole thing would take all night. The injections, for example."

"What injections?"

"Don't put on that innocent look! The cocaine..."

"Come on, I've told you a hundred times, cocaine is taken through the nose, not the needle. A pinch of white crystals on a nail file. Sniff and the deed is done."

"A pinch of white crystals on a nail file. Pierre, you're making fun of your mother. That's not right."

"I'm not making fun of you, I'm trying to tell you."

DIFFICULT DEATH

"Neither your insolence nor your lying will get the best of me. I know what I'm talking about. All those drugs are taken by injection."

"You know better than me, of course. I'm sure you've already shot coke."

Do you hear that? Pierre asking his mother if she has "shot coke." A son who dares imagine that his mother is now or ever was a cocaine addict! The ideal moment to repeat: "Pierre, you have lost all sense of respect."

Insolence has an answer to everything:

"How could I have retained any vestige of a sense of respect, living with a woman who spends her life jeering at a poor unfortunate man."

"A poor unfortunate man. Would you be speaking of your father, by any chance? How polite of you to say so in front of his wife, your mother. It certainly makes for an edifying tale: A certain gentleman drank and frequented houses of ill-fame, so long and hard that he lost his mind; and now his son, instead of taking stock and being inspired by such a sad example to choose a sensible, healthy way of life reaches the age of reason and simply laughs at his mother, rather than sympathizing with her, and of an individual whose excesses led him to a padded cell, remarks, 'He was a poor, unfortunate man.'"

As truly as a Barbedienne bronze surmounts the mantel in the Auteuil drawing room, an avenging Deity thrones on high in Whose name Mme. Dumont-Dufour is enabled to prophesy as of today that drugs and companions such as Bruggle can only produce – and soon – the same effect on this unfortunate child that excesses of an analogous albeit lesser order once brought down upon a certain Colonel of her acquaintance. Like father, like son…

From the prosecuting attorney impersonation the daughter of the late Justice Dufour shifts to her stationmaster voice:

"All aboard for Ratapoilopolis!"

Pierre's jaw tightens.

Once more he is being shown the rails down which he will roll to the asylum. "All aboard for Ratapoilopolis!" His teeth grind together. He makes no reply to the exultant Mme. Dumont-Dufour but silently repeats to himself that he is indeed the son of a man who wished to attach palm leaves to the wheels of cannons in order to convert them into "fish-cannoneers." That in itself is to his mother the ultimate criterion whereby – until the end of time, should Pierre, fate willing, sire offspring – the insanity of Dumont's descendants will be measured.

Insanity.

Mme. Dumont-Dufour does not miss a single one of the contractions that twist Pierre's face.

Insanity, which she dispenses, as it were, like a drug put up in individual doses of misfortune with which from her Auteuil apartment she bombards – wham, bam ! you asked for it, you got it – men who deceived their wives or drank too much Amer Picon and young people who enjoy cocktails and come home after midnight.

Indeed, she is not far from thinking that if the Colonel is in an asylum today it is only right she should have gotten this modest quid pro quo for all the mean tricks he played on her. Hence the sovereign manner and superior air with which from her easy chair she announces in stationmaster tones: "All aboard for Ratapoilopolis!"

Ratapoilopolis?

Pierre's jaws tighten to the breaking point. His eyes stare and see nothing, can no longer see a thing. The thin-lipped woman facing him knows what she wants. She is about to prove to her son that he is a degenerate, for even if she has renounced her own share of worldly happiness, she certainly has a right to something in the way of compensation, doesn't she? Hence her style of handing down edicts, her habit of infallibility. She would break her neck were she obliged to construct reasoned arguments and seek out proofs in support of every last thing she says. But with Pierre there is no need to exhaust oneself; he's not too sharp, poor boy. A couple of well-placed words and you have got him. It does him no good to talk big, discourse of all manner of things, pass judgment on God and the Devil, or hang out with Americans,

DIFFICULT DEATH

Czechoslovakians, Yugoslavians, and a horde of others like them, or drug himself, get drunk, demolish coat racks, and be friends with a whole raft of little horrors, he comes through it all with a transparent honesty which Justice Dufour's fair daughter, that implacable avenger, can always turn to her own best advantage.

She had only to pronounce the word Ratapoilopolis for Pierre to clench his teeth. A job well begun is soon done. She watches him unwaveringly, despite increasing darkness, making no move to turn on the light. Darkness, she well knows, can be an ally. Snugly ensconced in her armchair, she waits for Pierre to swamp and founder in his thoughts.

Abnormal, degenerate, or insane?

Should the fact that his body isn't bulging with muscles and that love and its games are cutting his will power and sanity to shreds alarm him?

Yet he had never known the insanity of arrogance, or presumed to repudiate his portion of banal conformity. All he wanted was to be another face in the crowd, nothing more. He hoped for no greater happiness than that of mingling his soul with those of others in an anonymous continent up and down the coasts of which his eyes and ears would be like ports open to the eyes and ears of all mankind. His own thoughts, his own nerve-ends, were they the brightest corals of the spirit and flesh, amounted to so little in relation to the whole. No more than a peninsula, not even that, a mere antenna rates the name Pierre Dumont and experiences the surprises of this singular ocean. But out of the sea of adventures has come a fleet of guilty boats which even now his blood is sweeping along in quest of he knows not what harbor. Mangled thoughts, shapeless desires, garbled secrets – are all these heading for some less-than-final shipwreck?

Insanity?

Ratapoilopolis?

Pierre grows desperate, tears well up in his eyes, he chokes with remorse over things for which he himself is in no way to blame. He feels he is the shadow of a monster and, like all shadows, doomed to exaggerate even further the deformities of the creature it projects. His father? A lunatic? What sun of despair made him an extension of that demented man? An invisible link connects him with that traveler to Ratapoilopolis, who within another two months will have written the same letter to Mme. de Pompadour fifteen hundred times. A photograph of his subconscious mind, "and a lot of good that does us," Mme. Dumont-Dufour invariably adds when asked. A photograph of his subconscious: Isn't it all too true that certain of Pierre's temptations and ways of putting things coincide with certain of the Colonel's in exactly the same fashion as the letters coincide with one another?

"You are the spitting image of your father," Mme. Dumont-Dufour infallibly repeats, apparently only to be doubly sure of poisoning Pierre's mind and at the same time to work herself up into a rage.

"You're the spitting image of your father." In one short sentence she discovers her prospects of revenge on a whole world from which she has derived neither joy nor ecstasy, and more especially on both Colonel Dumont, whom she was forced for such a long time to endure, and Pierre, who is the opposite of what she appreciates, namely herself.

Again and again she tells herself it would be stupid indeed to forgo the one and only real pleasure that ever came her way, that of inflicting revenge on her son for his father's misdeeds. Pierre, who relates to his archetype, Hippolytus, in the same way as a photograph relates to its negative, will expiate another's sins. He understands his role so well that he lets his mother talk on without turning a hair, or at most offers a whimsical rebuttal when she attacks him, as if he were not actually accountable for his own actions, or in fact as if he took no interest in a life he was being called upon to justify. On the other hand, whenever the Colonel's name comes up, he has always sought excuses and extenuating circumstances with a stubbornness that he was the first to admit was naïve and childish. In this he was not defending the errors of Pierre Dumont but those of his father, which, as he well knew, he was being made to inherit solely in order to be held responsible for them. But regardless of the inevitable outcome, he considered there could be nothing more cowardly than to refuse to answer in that unhappy man's name and place when he was being arraigned without any means of conducting his own defense. Colonel Dumont's life had furnished the child Pierre with his first notions of wrongdoing, and the only way he could justify its disorders was to plead insanity. And plead insanity he did, which is why he attempted in all seriousness to explain to Mme. Dumont-Dufour the torments suffered by a man who feels his sanity slipping away from him. But Pierre is a poor actor. He is incapable of taking advantage of the role, and it exhausts him. He is deeply moved by his own eloquence, which does not have the luck to touch Mme. Dumont-Dufour at all, and − because he is unwilling to confine himself to empty phrases − he unwittingly sets out on the highroad to Ratapoilopolis, only to perceive en route that the torments he is describing could quite easily bear the name of Pierre Dumont. He finds himself in a hellish landscape, a mass of twisted flames through which he must struggle, cut off from the hope of a simple guiding light.

He calls himself an imbecile, a ham actor. Worst of all, some of the hellfire, despite the flickering of its flames, iluminates him with sufficient clarity to see in a flash that the answers he is giving Mme. Dumont-Dufour in the Colonel's name are actually being given less in his father's behalf than against his mother, and that this is not a matter of obedience to some feeling of filial love or respect, but rather one of contempt and hatred which is a reflection of the contempt and hatred which Mme. Dumont-Dufour (no doubt unconsciously) heaps on a son whose mere presence represents an extension of the man she has come to loathe, never having tried to love or even understand him.

Therefore it is a duel.

On the defensive, having had neither the choice of weapons nor the advantage of the opening attack, Pierre desperately attempts to prove to Mme. Dumont-Dufour that if she has suffered misfortunes it is only because she deserved them and brought them on herself in the first place. Pierre has a number of precise and direct moves, but even as he perceives that Mme. Dumont-

RENE CREVEL

Dufour is going pale he says to himself that his powers for evil have their limits – more than once he has felt the menace emanating from their source, and now remembers all the times he has been obliged, in order to forget just a bit, to force upon himself long bouts of work or sex, long walks, even drinking and drugs. And no sooner had this inexorably imposed constraint taken effect – as it invariably did when he came home – than Mme. Dumont-Dufour, in one of the scenes she excelled at setting in motion upon any pretext great or small, would deftly contrive to make him feel that he would indeed fall into the trammels of that hell whose delirium and terrors he himself seeks to conjure up in order to throw his mother's mind into confusion and touch her heart. Queen of her Auteuil drawing room as was Lucretia of her crag, Mme. Dumont-Dufour looks down from afar on a sea of insanity and laughs to see ships in distress. She has central heating, hot and cold water, a bathroom, electricity, gas, an elevator, a dumbwaiter. As she had been wont to say each time the Colonel went on some new fling, of which the garrison ladies made no great effort to spare her any of the details: "He who laughs last laughs best." Mme. Dumont-Dufour wept more than once. It never occurred to her that it was purely out of rage. Today she unseals her lips and laughs heartily, while the Colonel in his padded cell makes friends with a straitjacket.

. And Pierre, that spoiled brat, not only defends his father but pushes insolence to the point of threatening his own mother: "You call yourself a Christian...Hell..."

"Hell," indeed. Mme. Dumont-Dufour laughs her head off. Pierre talking about Hell, Pierre who never sees the inside of a church, ignores Lent, although his self-sacrificing mother bled herself white to put him through the best Catholic school, Pierre talking about Hell because his mother is supposedly lacking in Christian charity – it's a scream. First let him respect his mother as she herself respected her father, Justice Dufour. Then we'll see.

Mme. Dumont-Dufour gets carried away in a gale of contemptuous hilarity and bitter jibes. She lets go like a true virtuoso, an artiste, without for a moment losing her sang-froid which permits

40

DIFFICULT DEATH

her both to organize the victory and enjoy it, pulling out all the stops but one, her self-control; whereas Pierre always goes off at a tangent, suicidally, which invariably lands him up, as it were, in the middle of a swamp at midnight, in Ratapoilopolis.

She savors her triumph in all of its different nuances and in front of her vanquished offspring tastes the joys of a hateful passion, so visibly incestuous, so transparently and malignantly directed against her own son, that the latter is startled to find himself murmuring a verse, which he had never understood when assigned to memorize it at school, from Racine:

I fled him, yet he followed in disguise,
And seemed to watch me from his father's eyes...

His father's eyes.

A resemblance excites Mme. Dumont-Dufour much as a red cape does a bull. Even if Pierre had had nothing in common with Colonel Dumont, either in appearance or personality, the mere fact of hearing so much talk about the Colonel would have made him wonder what similarities might exist between the two of them. Or he might simply have taken to mimicking the Colonel unconsciously; for in a family where a certain personality has become predominant by reason of its good or bad qualities, if the tastes or obsessions which have been subjects of amazement are transmitted, and if the children are caricatures or "spitting images" of the personality that has occupied the center of the stage, whether to the others' benefit or at their expense, this is less to be attributed to blood, heredity, or any other so-called natural force than to the action exercised by the talk of those who witnessed the great man, were he a criminal, a genius, or merely a crank.

So it is that in every family there arises a folklore whose protagonists are the symbols of such and such tendencies, and so it is that children may be poisoned by an oral tradition, unless their own innate energies are more powerful than those of the persons about whom they are told, or ready-made models are unconsciously offered to be imitated.

Take the example of Mme. Blok, who, unlike Mme. Dumont-Dufour, has no malevolent designs. Despite all of her own efforts

41

and Bricoulet's gallant attentions, she never manages to stop thinking about M. Blok's suicide and talking about it to her daughter. Unable to forget her husband's death, she not only bemoans her own lot but feels sorry for Diane, whom she imagines doomed to an imminent self-inflicted end. Yet, moronically obvious as it might seem, Mme. Blok would no doubt be amazed if one told her that by dint of all this chatter of suicide, Diane might well end up like her father. At the moment, still thunderstruck at the family destiny, Mme. Blok is not far from seeing in Diane an Iphigenia whose corpse will be brought home one day from Montparnasse, a hole drilled in her temple, her throat cut, or her body blue with poison from head to toe. And so, in the little drawing room on avenue d'Orléans where early each afternoon the girl packs up her paints, brushes, and pencils before leaving for art class, the coffee hour is filled with a monotonous lamentation followed by the eternal recommendation, "Watch out for the traffic, little girl, and above all, Diane, don't let yourself slip into a morbid frame of mind. Think of your mama. If you died, I'd be all alone in the world. Don't follow your poor father's example. Oh, why didn't I pay attention to my poor grandmother, the one who lived on rue de Grenelle-Saint-Germain and married a redhead. She was a dear, and she warned me when I was getting married. I can still hear her repeating it over and over to me: Suicide runs in the Blok family and suicide is like carrot-heads. When it runs in a family it's there for good. The best you can hope for is that it will skip a generation or two."

Diane has already put on her hat. "See you, Mother." Mme. Blok allows her to leave only after she has sworn that she will never under any circumstances commit suicide. Diane laughs and swears: "Cross my heart and hope to die!" She is halfway down the stairs and her mother, leaning over the banister, advises, "And above all, don't let yourself slip into one of your morbid moods!"

But it does Diane little good to laugh at the grandmother in the rue de Grenelle-Saint-Germain and her theory of suicide and red hair (which is precisely what her dear mother, Herminie, did back in the days when she was bent on marrying Dimitri Blok in

DIFFICULT DEATH

defiance of everything and everyone). It not only does Diane no good to laugh, but often she comes to look on suicide as a definite threat against which no precaution would be excessive. Moreover, this threat takes on the character of a promise at times; and on more than one day of anxiety or depression, or even simply nervous fatigue, she finds the idea of certain self-destructive acts as inviting as a cool, deep doorway in a street sweltering under a noonday sun. At such moments she cannot think about anything without concluding, "It's not for nothing that we live on the sixth floor," or "Guns aren't just for stray dogs." Actually, however, Diane has good color, good muscle tone, and a good appetite, so that poisonous thoughts such as "It's not for nothing that we live on the sixth floor," or "Guns aren't just for stray dogs," and others of the same stripe, instead of doing her in, have on her the effect of an inoculation. In this manner, germs one might initially have feared as deadly protect from the very death they bear. This does not prevent a slight fever, actually, an onset in miniature, from appearing, for a time at least, in those who have been emotionally or otherwise vaccinated.

Mme. Blok and Mme. Dumont-Dufour's remarks on suicide and madness have thus made of Diane and Pierre a brother-and-sister pair whose bonds of acquired kinship were unusually strong from the start, because Diane's anxieties had just become pronounced and Pierre's were growing by leaps and bounds.

But Mme. Blok's obsession was an uninspired one. A hackneyed tale unenlivened with the slightest variation, it was not hard to get used to. In the end, Diane no longer even heard her mother's plaintive and monotonous litanies.

So, instead of trembling at the Blok family curse, beneath which her mother already pictured Diane's shoulders bowed, she has in time straightened up and remembered that it's healthier to breathe through your nose. Every morning she opens her window and cleanses her lungs with the bracing air of a quiet neighborhood, which she likes to imagine is the same as country air. What difference does it make at that point, if Mme. Blok for the thousandth time describes her drawing room as it was that fateful evening,

43

the guests, her dress, her stockings, her shoes, and recites the menu and wine list of the dinner she had been about to give that night when poor Dimitri in his broad-checked trousers and shirt-sleeves – while for the past hour...And may the good Lord have mercy on the insanity of such an act and not refuse this husband and father who lost his head admission into Heaven which as we know is closed to those who choose a self-inflicted passing... When he *ought* to have been dressed...

"Tra-la-la-lal-la..." Diane sings to herself, not intending any inso-lence thereby, but only because she is young, loves to eat fruit, prefers lemonade to vodka or even champagne, and enjoys day-dreaming about mountain trails at nightfall or the pleasant smell of seawater drying on her swimmer's arms in summer sunlight. And she kisses the skin over her biceps of which she is quite proud. But the skin she is kissing no longer tastes of salt, it is Paris skin. Right now she is on her way to the studio, tonight to a café in Montparnasse, tomorrow to a dance, a benefit for some Russian or other, and the day after tomorrow...She tells herself that every bit of it would be an insufferable bore if Pierre...She stops right there. Neither working nor going to parties is any fun without Pierre. Yet there are others who are more reliable and even more charming than this capricious, surly, overgrown boy. So what? Al-ready she is thinking about the consolation she will be providing him today. Already she forgets her own happiness, her simple happiness at being alive, in order to feel sorry for Pierre who is perpetually wretched. His heart is always too hot or too cold, and something almost physical – he can feel it so distinctly at the very core of his being – makes his heart palpitate in terror like the soles of one's feet at the edge of a cliff, and not because his heart is hard but because it exaggerates; thus winter freezes it to the cracking point and summer makes it burst into flames.

Pierre's hands often tremble, and he is at times unable to swal-low even a scrap of bread. He envies Diane's rosy cheeks, appetite, and above all, calm.

For him, each day involves eluding some new trap contrived by Mme. Dumont-Dufour with a genius as versatile as it is implacable.

DIFFICULT DEATH

Under an eye that knows every trick in the book, he feels himself therefore ready to surrender from one moment to the next and keeps on telling himself that since he'll never get rid of the thing haunting him, it would doubtless be better to abandon himself to it right away.

Why hold back, torture oneself, be torn up inside?

He takes showers, goes on long walks every day, refrains from compressing his lips, and tests syllogisms in order to lend a complexion of sanity to his fantasies, and yet this lamp (it's always the same, never changes) burns perpetually in the darkness behind the windows of his soul, where it corrupts the sun and rots the heavens.

The lamp's stubborn though anxious flame wavers but never ceases to illuminate an obscene black mass that is being celebrated on an altar of bones somewhere inside him. Pierre burns with shame at the faces, the bodies his sleep invents to torture him in the dark.

Should he run away? Or cry out for help?

He murmurs a name: "Diane."

Diane.

How it would simplify matters if she would agree never to leave him! She alone knows how to summon up words that soothe and ward off sadness. Her ways of being sweet are precise, her intentions exact; she is aware of every sort of consolation from the greatest down to the smallest. Thus, having proved to Pierre that he has no reason to imagine himself doomed to insanity merely because the Colonel has written Mme. de Pompadour the same letter a thousand times over, she leads him to a place where the shade of three trees darkens the river bank, creating a coolness for which a harshly glaring sun had made one thirst. In wintertime, she heads straight for the streets one should take in order to avoid the needles of the wind and of the heart. If Pierre decides to go to the theater, she has only to glance at the Morris pillar to tell him how far he can rely on the multicolored promises whose mosaic tempted them; and that if he goes to such and such a play, whose title in flowery black on green or red lettering had initially beguiled them, their evening would be a complete washout; whereas in a theater almost next door they are playing a foreign playwright, unknown to the theater-going public, despised by the critics and the snobs, whose three acts (which they just happen to be putting on tonight) will enchant Pierre.

Diane knows everything, at least everything Pierre ought to be doing, seeing, hearing, and reading in order to be happy. Diane is Pierre's better, more sensible half. He is moved to tears at the thought of her. He imagines he has at last found happiness.

Then why does he suddenly shrug his shoulders? Why does he scorn the very idea of Diane as one's better half?

Yes, this very morning, from the depths of his last nightmares, those nightmares at dawn whose shadow stains the whole day, he was calling her with words of fire; to subdue the pitfalls of unconsciousness, he was already calling her his better half while still asleep. But now he is awake, he can't help wondering if, once having entered into the sole possession and enjoyment of this better half, he would love her so much, need her presence so badly, or even feel like seeing her at all? Having calmed himself down, does he truly still wish she would stay with him forever? If he asks himself such questions, isn't it because he is already anticipating times when he will have to continue to put up with her without feeling any spontaneous urge to have her around? The two of them will be bound only by ties of mutual gratitude, and he hates being bound by any duty, least of all by the duty of gratitude.

Moreover, Diane knows him (he is unwilling to admit she loves him) to the point of discerning the slightest changes in his heart and mind, and she never fails to be affected by any that are not in her favor. Pierre recalls a sad face that has often made him hate himself, as well as certain temptations he had hitherto indulged but for which there remained no excuse, once her unhappiness deprived them of the slightest legitimate grounds.

He would prefer any form of suffering to the shame of those days when Diane, after hours spent making him feel better, felt she was no longer needed, and felt it so acutely that he himself suffered more remorse over his own indifference than he would have for an actual crime.

Diane had stood up and, although wanting to stay, had gone through the motions of leaving. Feeling utterly obligated to detain her, Pierre begged her not to go away. He asked her to put her hands on his forehead, which felt feverish, it being late afternoon. She obeyed with a joy that she made no effort to conceal. Her fingers found their accustomed place around a head from which their palpable coolness had more than once expelled the tiny voodoo-dolls of woe. But Pierre, who no longer had any need for a healing touch and was growing exasperated at not finding it so pleasurable that he would want it to continue for its own sake, thought of those drawings in the newspaper advertising section in which one sees a good genie bearing the name of one or another painkiller, who with his magic magnet frees people's heads of the nails driven into them by neuralgia, migraine headache, or even simple indigestion; for as soon as he is happy, as soon as he feels strong, Diane's hand on his forehead is a useless compress.

Diane's hand, a useless compress?

"Egotist," he thinks and reproaches himself for having wronged the only creature who loves him; at the same time, he admits that if things did go further with her he would value her no more than he would some drug or medication, and he is ashamed. He is ashamed not only of having dissembled with one who means him well and does him good, but also – and above all – of feeling empty and not knowing what actions or words will save him from the boredom by which he feels threatened.

He is paralyzed in a ridiculous posture.

Is he therefore a professional complainer, and on top of that, one as narrowly specialized as his mother Mme. Dumont-Dufour, who has nothing to say once she has finished enumerating her reasons for anger and vengeance?

Thanks to Diane he has calmed down and is at peace. But instead of rejoicing in this calm, he appears to resemble those mediocrities who can produce flights of the most uncanny eloquence as long as some indisposition animates their delirium, but once they feel better have nothing to say outside of pompous clichés.

Tongue-tied, Pierre reminds himself that his silence must not last any longer. He says something at random. It rings false. He attempts a full-length sentence. The best that honesty permits him to invent is: "I don't mean to send you home, sweetheart, but your mother must be expecting you for dinner."

"You're right, Pierre. I'll go now."

Both stand up.

Diane asks, "What are you doing after dinner? Who are you going out with?"

In response, Pierre names a name, always the same:

"Bruggle."

"You're seeing him every night?"

"God knows I have few enough friends. Arthur is one of the very few who really like me."

"You haven't always seemed so sure of that."

"We've had our bad moments. He's nervous, too sensitive, but I am as sure of the affection he has for me as I am of mine for him. How about you?"

Diane says nothing but tries to make her lips smile. Uncertainty makes them curl instead, and at the same time wrinkles her eyelids, between which her eyes shine brilliantly. Pierre thinks, "Someone must have told her Arthur and I..." He hopes for tears, observes that Diane is jealous, and wonders, "Is the jealousy from love or wounded pride?" Then, once more, he feels ashamed of himself.

Actually, her jealousy is both at once, love and wounded pride, but for the small pleasure of playing games is he going to keep inflicting pain on his sole source of peace? He is aware that if Mme. Dumont-Dufour unleashes a new scene, or if Bruggle stands him up tonight or wounds him with one of those remarks or pointed silences he wields with the cruel and sure grace of a young animal, the first thing tomorrow morning he will be on the telephone begging Diane to have lunch with him or meet him

DIFFICULT DEATH

around two o'clock in some Left Bank café from which they will set out on a consolatory walk along the Seine.

Pierre calls himself a cad, digs his nails into his palms to punish himself, swears never, never again to treat Diane in this hateful fashion; and, because he is unwilling to see the tears that may be forthcoming thanks to him, his lips kiss both her eyes, and Diane forgets his impatient gestures, his curt replies, and above all his tone of voice when speaking of Bruggle and relating (and in the process exaggerating) instances of the latter's malice towards him. He had no need to spell it out so carefully, for her to understand, and suffer. Yet Diane not only excuses Pierre, she even manages to find new reasons to feel sorry for him and love him all the more. "Poor kid," she thinks, "how that Bruggle makes him suffer, with all those whims and affectations." Then she completely pardons Pierre whose mouth, softened by remorse, she feels against her eyelashes. Then, although she had no need to catch him unawares to know he blushed with shame, she raised her head and told the boy, "You judge yourself too harshly, Pierre. You're a much better person than you think."

Yet, even if Pierre is better than he thinks and is being too harsh on himself, she privately thinks that she and she alone is to blame. In Diane's opinion, the young Dumont's entire moral outlook is distorted by his overestimation of herself. Thus he so often and so harshly denounces his own weaknesses only because he believes Diane to be a paragon of wholesomeness and well-being, a belief that makes him more severely neurotic than ever. Diane thus reaches the point of getting angry with herself for having strength that can be neither a blessing nor a virtue when it becomes so brutally obvious that she can no longer come to the rescue of the person needing her help without intimidating him and giving him an even more disagreeable idea of himself than he already had.

And so it comes about that Diane no longer wants Pierre to think her a stranger to sin, or so pure and strong-willed as never to have had the slightest reason to reproach herself in the most

49

secret recesses of her mind or body. Bringing her face close to his, she mimics desire, and pretends she can no longer resist a thirst that has overmastered her senses, her entire being, from her hands trembling on the boy's shoulders to her bosom heaving like the ocean in a storm, eyes closed, nostrils flaring, and neck thrown back in an attitude of languorous abandon designed to make Pierre think she is yielding to temptation, as her gently pursed lips suddenly blow up like a balloon and glue themselves onto the young man's mouth.

But how could one not see, in those too widely parted lips, that it was not a matter of lust but instead of a desire to give the impression of lustfulness? In his turn Pierre is touched. He understands that Diane wants to make him imagine that she, too, lusts after warm skin, teeth, and all the rest, and has never hesitated to take advantage of every chance to enjoy them that she gets. And so this well-contrived demonstration of sensuality proves, contrary to what Diane had expected, that she is not accustomed to offering her lips and that, even to Pierre, she gave them less out of curiosity or the hope of pleasure than from pure, simple, friendly charity.

Pierre thus understands that she is attached to him and that in order to avoid his putting a distance between them (Pierre knows moreover that Diane has such faith in him and in his affection that she thinks only his conscience could definitively lead him to break off their relationship) she would even gladly consent to appear to him, as well as to others no doubt, as a girl who has already started "running around." Her first priority is that Pierre should never have to blush in front of her, and to that end, not only would she consent to pass for a flirt, a good-time girl, a flapper, a hot number, even if need be an ex-virgin, but in addition she keeps repeating to herself a resolution to be endlessly patient, come what may, telling herself for instance that she will pay no mind to gossip, either at art school or among friends. At the same time, she seeks to ignore the evidence, and forget even the name, of the lithe and lightfooted Bruggle, and with her cool touch to reduce (as if they were so many swellings) all the multicolored temptations, qualms, and obsessions which encircle Pierre with a rainbow of sadness.

The clear inexperience of Diane's first kiss forced Pierre to perceive all the intentions of a tenderness so generously bestowed on him, and the honesty, at once discreet and passionate, that shone through it all plunged him into new depths of remorse, the very idea of which had hitherto been inconceivable to him. He imagined himself to be captivated, a prisoner of love, and often repeated to himself that the greatest gift a woman or a girl could give a man was precisely such an angelic kiss which out of charity feigned the behavior of a whore.

An angel who out of charity played the whore? He accused himself of romanticism, but nonetheless repeated, with a kind of mystical fervor, this set phrase that kept him on the verge of tears while holding Diane in his arms, kissing the nape of her neck and repeating, "Diane, Diane baby," in the tone of a sinner who would thank his patron saint for appearing in an hour of most heartfelt remorse, were the saint simply to tell his own life story, embellishing it with faults identical to those committed by the lowliest and guiltiest of creatures, only in order to make it clear that even quasi-ethereal beings have known temptations, and yielded to them, before at last reaching the felicity and peace of Heaven.

"Diane, Diane baby," he repeated, and there was such a fervor in his voice the girl thought they might be on the point of advancing from luminous camaraderie to amorous enchantment. Pierre himself (though he knew he was incapable of making sacrifices for Diane equivalent to those he made for Bruggle every day) wondered whether he had not reached the zenith of true love, since he was deifying Diane – whereas he had no need of Heaven to exalt his taste and need for Bruggle – since he felt himself quite ready to forget that this sweet and simple girl, whom he had gotten to know at a Montparnasse art school and at painters' dances, who was neither prudish nor vulgar, neither allowing herself to be tempted nor shocked, was incapable of tarnishing herself by a single gesture, word, or step, so that he almost had to think she represented some imponderable principle and not the common run of humanity, which smelt simultaneously of madness, terror, and tears.

"Diane, Diane baby," he kept repeating and would not once allow himself to think of her as the daughter of M. Blok who had hanged himself in his broad-checked trousers and the fat, soft, tearful Mme. Blok.

And so, only a few minutes after having thought that Diane was, all in all, nothing but a useless compress, he was obliged to admit to himself that if she had cured him, it had not come about by means of a specific act of assistance or an action like that ascribed to medications, but by means of a miracle whose virtue she bore in herself, which made her entire being shine with a grace so mysterious one was suddenly forced to call it divine.

Then he decided it would be best to ask Diane to live with him for the rest of his life, an arrangement from which she would infallibly derive great joy and he great peace – but as soon as he tried to form a precise picture of a fate which Diane's kindness alone allowed him to embroider upon, he was already losing confidence rapidly, postponing till later, asking nothing, and at the very instant he was repeating to Diane that he adored her, he remembered that the afternoon they had just spent together had provided him with a glimpse of what the less than divine part of their shared existence would be like.

The thought of it filled him with tenderness at first – he would forget the Colonel and his insanity, Mme. Dumont-Dufour and her implacable vengeance. He would spend peaceful nights after fearless days. A fresh, docile body cuddled up next to him would bring sleep without nightmares in a double bed. Even in the middle of his dreams, he would no longer remember those solitary walks he had used to pursue until dawn in the streets of a city where passing strangers recovered their wild animal eyes.

He would forget Bruggle, his irresistible whims, and the endless adventures on which he dragged Pierre as if for the pleasure of imagining him the morning after, ravaged by alcohol, disgust, and fear. If he lived with Diane, all the troubles and sadnesses of that previous life would be erased from memory. He would be

DIFFICULT DEATH

happy, so happy he would no longer feel himself. But already Pierre despises the whole idea, almost laughs out loud at the mere thought of it. Diane puts on her fur. He escorts her to the door and lets her leave without a word. Diane and Pierre? Their happiness together? Come on, now! A lovesong that would amount to little more than the whistling of a tea kettle.

If Pierre loved Diane less he would doubtless consent to make her his nurse, on condition he could dismiss her upon recovery. Then Diane could remember that suicide is like carrot-heads. Red hair and suicide in the Blok family? Pierre foresees Diane's death, accepts it, decides on it. Has he in fact gone insane, and not only insane but turned into an odious monster, a criminal, and is Mme. Dumont-Dufour right after all when she declares him to be endowed with the most vicious instincts? Diane is the only creature in whom he has invariably found a refuge. Of this he is well aware, so much so that he has created a whole mystique surrounding her. Yet, now, despite all that he owes her, he is prepared to think he just might systematically exploit her to the limit and then, having used her up, throw her out to die. Pierre calls himself a man but is, in fact, nothing but a child in the grip of a nightmare. After going to such lengths to abuse someone who helped him in his need, would he stop at anything? Then, indeed, remorse would get the better of him once and for all. Already he must beg Diane to forgive him his thoughts, Diane the wise virgin who goes everywhere and has never lost either her smile or her sketch book, Diane who is stronger than Pierre and has succeeded in escaping the intoxication of sorrows whose spectacle she witnessed at much too early an age, Diane the wise virgin who feels sorry for those addicted to drunkenness, parties, and the search for new vices. She knows Pierre would soon collapse if he had no one at his side to defend or assist him.

If he were by himself, he would not know which way to run. How many times has he gone out, sick of himself, not to call on another for help but to lose himself in the streets or some anonymous park, and, as he forced himself to believe, for the most beautiful of all promises? He walked on and on, but never found

53

that nameless, faceless dream in which he had decided to lose himself. He kept on walking. No one's eyes held his own. On the wet ground the least glimmer of light multiplied all sadness. He kept walking and the cold clung to him like a clammy bathing suit beneath his clothes and underclothes. His teeth chattered. His bones suffered in solitude, every last one of them; for his bones had already devoured his flesh. That part of his body still capable of giving pleasure shrank and drooped. In his pockets his hands were sapless, colorless flowers. At such moments he went in any-where, not in the hope of finding any specific human help, for if he sought to postpone the imminent breakdown, it was by a strange means – he would have no idea what to do had he been confronted by a body inhabited by a mind similar to his own. He remembers. One closes one's eyes, breathes, swallows no matter what, and after ten minutes one need no longer fear to open one's eyes, for a new world is bursting into flower over the wreckage of the old.

The body is no longer a bundle of flesh condemned to misfor-tune, the body is no longer cold. It leaps, flies, weighs no more than a song under the midnight sun.

The midnight sun!

Alas, the clock just sounded seven o'clock. Pierre must remem-ber that he is in an Auteuil drawing room, a small drawing room where he continues to sit unmoving, as a pair of eyes subject him to the most rigorous examination. There is no more kindness left on earth tonight. Even the street must be exaggerating the cruelty of it all by not offering a single one of its promises, magnets for wet, tired feet in unadventurous late-afternoon shoes. And the gaslights that wink mockingly. Pierre is used to the tiny stars they scatter over the pavement when the sidewalk no longer takes on the sheen of some redemptive temptation to eyes heavy with re-morse. Mute and paralysed in an armchair, a circle of shadow round him like a suffocating mass of cotton wadding, he no longer even wishes to flee this house and its watchful eyes.

He would never be able to stand living like so many others he has seen, looking through their windows from outside, with their ceiling lamps whose light holds happy families at table in a green embrace. He laughs contemptuously. Dining room, ceiling lamps, happy families, green embrace. All it lacks is the soup tureen and what a lovely bouquet, dear. No, such things may be even nicer and more innocuous than a bunch of wildflowers, but he is not about to offer them to Diane.

Even in the splashes of pink and blue, glimpsed in the apartments of strangers, wherein are neither perils nor surprises, as someone picks out with one finger Clair de lune, resurrecting it with a multitude of other tunes that encourage people to rejoice and persevere in their simplicity, there are no harmonies so bland as to silence that other insidious music that starts softly, only the more horribly to snarl, then roar, then rush one and crush one's skull between its teeth. Pierre tells himself that, without in the least understanding how or why, he is condemned to have inflicted on himself a hellish orchestra whose every instrument is capable of creating new torture. Bows crossing his eyelids make of a simple teardrop a rich arpeggio, while Mme. Dumont-Dufour, stationmaster of woe, intones, "All aboard for Ratapoilopolis!"

Ratapoilopolis? Insanity? Again? Come, come! A stiff upper lip, please! Fists clenched, his nails dig into palms whose wetness is at last sure about something, and, from that small pang of certainty, Pierre will strive to be reborn within self-imposing limits. Already he wants to move faster than his thoughts, silence this damned muttering, forge ahead, raise his voice, be the master of his fate, that is, control everything inside and around himself and not allow dreams and images to catch him unawares unless he feels like it.

Feels like it? Thus he admits to a taste for certain nightmares... He admits but at the same time thinks that this honesty cannot fail to help him master himself; that moreover, because intelligent, he is far from being incapable of logic.

But a clever head is not necessarily airtight. Open to any wind after storms, his head in the morning is a fruit heavy with bitter dew, the dew of dreams.

Dreams.

He knows them all, from the ones that make you laugh to cer-

RENE CREVEL

tain ones that leave your face at dawn lined with the traces left by
tears, paths that lead nowhere. Half closing his eyes for a moment,
he already remembers how last night Mme. Dumont-Dufour in a
pink slip and a long mourning veil did cartwheels across the night
sky over Paris, and, shaking her legs (whose skinniness had always
seemed to her a sign of race), shouted with such vehemence that
one could have heard her from the Bastille to Porte-Maillot and
from Montmartre to Montrouge, "Go ahead and make a wish,
make a wish, I can lose a necklace and show my backside, too, I'm
a star, a shooting star!" But suddenly the shooting star vanishes,
and because he failed to make a wish, Pierre must needs walk in
darkness. He hears himself condemned to wander alone in the
Louvre until he retrieves his eyes which he negligently allowed
to drop out of their sockets, he's not sure exactly where, in the
feathers with which they have just filled all the galleries of the
museum. Tiny feathers stick to his lips, his nostrils, fill his empty
eyelids, and his mouth. He suffocates, tries to cry out, cannot, and
at last the blood he is weeping falls in drops so hot that the pain
of his scalded hands awakens him.

From bursts of laughter to an outburst of tears. From Mme.
Dumont-Dufour transmogrified into a comet in the sky over the
capital to the terror of one's own eyes being lost. Dreams. But
night does not contain them; their shadow stains his days. There
are, to be sure, quite a few traps one can fall into only when
asleep. For instance, when alone in bed, Pierre smothers himself
in the sheets and often cannot even find that life-buoy, the night
light. A cargo of unhappy flesh, the good ship *Pierre Dumont* is about
to go down with all hands. Let him disappear beneath the waves
and get it over with. That way at least there will be no shipwreck
on the shores of Ratapoilopolis.

Ratapoilopolis, shipwreck, waves. That would be too easy, too
good to be true. To disappear beneath the waves. Come on! Pierre
now realizes he is in a bed and will soon have to rise and get on
with the day's business.

Then he thinks of those mirrors in which, glimpsing himself,
he fails to recognize his own face and yet cannot but know that

DIFFICULT DEATH

the young man he is looking at bears the name of Pierre Dumont. And he pinches himself, but pinching fails to cause the pain it might have been natural to expect it would. If there were nothing but mirrors...Likewise, spiral staircases...One does not know where one is going. One goes up, down, one is frightened, one takes heart, when all of a sudden, one is eyeball to eyeball with an indeterminate creature which it is impossible to call human, even though it has a head, a body, two arms, two hands, two feet. And one has to walk upstairs backwards because the monster forces one to. But one has scarcely climbed three steps, when a certain tiny shudder, attached as tightly to one's vertebral column as the mistletoe to its oak, warns one of the presence of a creature quite as real and no less indeterminate than the first, and just as the first forced one to climb and indicated it would not desist, the second monster is about to force one to descend the same staircase. Prisoner of two equal and opposite forces, incapable of advancing or retreating but nevertheless pressed to do both, one can no longer do anything but let oneself be crushed while Mme. Dumont-Dufour in a frilled nightgown, pins and curlpapers, and wearing 1900-style high-buttoned boots, waves a tea-cloth like a flag and blows a penny whistle.

All aboard for Ratapoilopolis!

Ratapoilopolis. Insanity?

Well might he confess his weakness! The sad thing, he repeats, is that he loves Diane too much to require any real sacrifice of her, and she is the only one who could help him recover from all the terrors which he would like to call vain but to which (again and again he tells himself) he will finally succumb. Yes, the sad thing is that, loving Diane, a girl he has nicknamed without the slightest intention of going overboard on the romantic side, "Diane of the Quiet Hands," he is unwilling to use her as a nurse, and at the same time must needs admit he is incapable of living with her indefinitely or even having her around much at all, once restored to calm, whereas he could never do without Bruggle, although the latter is a perpetual source of fresh sorrows, nay, fresh tortures; and since he is unwilling to renounce either one, it seems to him that from the impossibility of choosing will result final and utter solitude. Incapable of enduring such an ordeal, he would in that case prefer to give up life itself.

But, suddenly, big words, pompous expressions such as "give up life itself" make Pierre stumble on the too-smooth-and-easy path that he would gladly have followed as far as the ocean of death or oblivion; and having stumbled, he is forced to recover a more precise degree of self-awareness, to take stock and tell himself that the danger may be rather in the way he sees his torment than in the pain itself, and he goes so far as to believe that it was only by means of a kind of bad faith that, using a few dreams and sensations, he constructed on the platform of the Colonel's insanity the future and probable insanity of Pierre Dumont.

And so, because he has no confidence in his thoughts, despite the excellent "head line" palm readers discern in him he turns to his body to find reasons for optimism, although he is the first to admit he is weak in the arms and chest. Besides, Mme. Dumont-Dufour never lets slip an opportunity to call him a shrimp; but — no matter — he would like to think his appearance isn't all that bad. Didn't that boxer, a real hunk who knew what he was talking about and better than Mme. Dumont-Dufour, say the first time he saw Pierre naked, "You're a strange little bird, but that's no reason to say you don't make the grade." After that general verdict, there were more detailed comments, all of them appreciative, the memory of which heightens the color of Pierre's cheeks without making him blush with shame.

That big guy and his compliments may have been ridiculous; but why, on the other hand, should he give credence to the opinions aired by Mme. Dumont-Dufour in front of a teapot? Yet didn't Pierre just lay everything on the line, merely because one ignorant bourgeois woman had asked another if her son was abnormal and the second ignorant bourgeois woman replied that he was simply a bit degenerate?

But since, unfortunately, there does exist a Mme. Dumont-Dufour, let her let her son be. And the latter tells himself it would

DIFFICULT DEATH

be best to treat such a mother with silent disdain – that would at least have the advantage of passing for simple coldness, or even a sort of respect. Besides, after sixteen-odd years of a daily and enforced study, doesn't he know her too well for him to get interested to the point of bearing her any ill will? If she were good-looking, or had some strangeness about her, there would be nothing astonishing about the attention he pays to her in spite of himself, but he has looked at her with sufficient attention to know all of her faults by heart, even down to those of her skin, which is so slack and coarse-textured he is convinced one could plant a flower or a little flag in every pore. Today, looking at her motionless in her armchair, he thinks that underneath the dress, which betrays no human contours, her body takes up no more room than a coat rack; Pierre has so much trouble imagining the actual presence, the possibility, even, of such a body that he is incapable of imagining himself as its issue and extension in posterity. Thus, for example, when his mother reproaches him for not loving his family, he says to himself he has no idea who he might call family, since the most elementary social hygiene requires that he isolate the Colonel in his insanity, whereas on the other hand, Mme. Dumont-Dufour is nothing but a household gadget, noisier and more of an encumbrance perhaps, but of the same sort on the whole as the coat rack of Moroccan copper plates devised by her.

His mother's passion (it is a passionate hatred, to be sure, but passion nonetheless) he has never truly reciprocated with any emotion having its own internal dynamic, and his anger toward her is only just that of a person who, convinced of his own intelligence, has through weakness allowed the malignant aggressiveness of a creature he had never imagined to amount to anything more or better than an object to assert itself to the detriment of his own freedom and happiness, having from an early age imagined that indifference was of all attitudes the only possible one to take toward such a creature.

Besides, was this indifference not the veil of tranquility that shielded Pierre's earliest years in life? Only later did it seem to him the opposite of what it ought to be, and he was troubled, and

59

even went so far as to wonder whether his eyes and ears and that hidden sixth sense that allowed him to cherish the invisible world (which in child's language he called his "heart") were not the eyes, ears, and heart of a little monster, because, having heard the servants talk on certain subjects, when he tried to pin down that mysterious attraction which, according to the cook, a woman could not fail to exercise on a man, he never succeeded in believing that his own mother could have displayed any such charm or been able, through any detail of her body or mind, to interest the man he knew was his father, the man he was destined to become. Moreover, with regard to his mother's breast, he never experienced any of those feelings of curiosity that kept him swooning over the corsages of visiting ladies whose hands the Colonel loved to kiss slowly, inhaling their fragrance, nor any of those sweet pangs that pulled him up short on the sidewalk at the sight of the tight-fitting jackets of the flower-girls selling violets in the streets in wintertime. (He had called them "gypsies" in the red balloon era of his life.)

Thus, at a later date, when a boxer whom Pierre had met in a bar (he offered him lessons in "physical culture" with a smile whose double meaning Pierre had not spontaneously understood) told him, "You're a strange little bird but that's no reason to say you don't make the grade," and thereupon this Hercules with a pug nose and pink cheeks tried to make the little bird sing to a pizzicato accompaniment that was certainly not recommended by any treatise on breathing exercises or manual of calisthenics, the boy, at first amazed at the warmth of his own response to the other's tender and precise brutalities, suddenly thought that Mme. Dumont-Dufour's body and mannerisms had ended up making him sensitive to the least imperfections of the so-called fair sex, to the point that the joys of which this athlete was giving him a first inkling seemed to his body more natural than the others which, despite the disillusionment of certain nights spent in bed with women, he had persisted in believing to be the highest, nay, the only joys of love.

From that time on, if he was still capable of being aroused more than once by a woman's warmth, it was more in response to the warmth than to the woman; and as he allowed himself to be aroused without any longer seeking to value the object of his excitement, he expressed his urges with doglike brutalities whose insistent frenzy, which partners at first mistook for passion, soon gave way to such disgust that the bed was quickly deserted. And so, in a very short time, he was no longer in the slightest way tempted by the mere idea of young female flesh.

However, because he remembered the things the athlete had done, together with the possibilities of happiness he had deduced from them, he had come to look on young men with a more than comradely fondness, and at art school for instance, during the drawing class, in order to forget the ill-favored scullery maid who served as the model, it amused him to imagine, in place of this nudity of papier-mâché mammaries and buttocks, the boy sitting next to him, who, he could not help remarking to himself, had a fine leg, a slim waist, and a perfect torso. As for the fat model, in whom there had never been any question of discerning a creature susceptible of being desired, kissed, touched, Pierre was incapable of recognizing in her the slightest dignity of life beyond the simple interest value of a thing to be drawn, and he even went so far as to forget her altogether on her stage, and let her melt, decompose, while his fingers, spontaneously and unbidden by any look or thought, discovered on the paper a human continent whose ideal beaches his pencil traced in simple lines. His eyes, his nose, his mouth, and all that was flowering in him for happiness and unease had no other need or wish than to explore the secret of these invented maps, their peninsulas, their plains. The gaze of the young stranger sitting in the next seat held him as one ensnared, a prisoner.

But something said to someone else and overheard, or a glance at some neighbor's sketchpad, would suddenly force Pierre to remember the model, and he would reproach himself for having no self-control and readily accused his pencil of having betrayed, when it had in fact revealed, him. He decided to do violence to his nature and start the sketch over again, but it was no use trying to resuscitate the fat model – her existence remained too improbable; for, to his dazzlement, in mid-air as it were, between them, him and her, in a blaze of light transcending any bodily detail whatever, there exploded Youth in all its shining savagery.

After class, Diane – who had observed him from the back of the room – asked why he had paid so little attention to the model. He replied, "The child Septentrion danced two days and pleased." Diane recalled that only the day before they had sworn never to keep secrets from one another, but it did not occur to her to reproach this violation of their little treaty. She contented herself with the vague answer and did not venture to notice that it was obviously an evasion. Pierre, a bit ashamed of himself but lacking strength to admit or even say anything further, attempted a smile but his lips had such difficulty spreading in a facsimile of joy or happiness one would have thought they had been sliced apart by a superfine, perfectly horizontal wire.

Then his voice took on the gentle tones of one who has much to be forgiven for, and he offered to walk her home, pressed her arm tightly inside his own, but could not make her the gift of his heart and mind, which he could feel slipping away into a haze, though he was not quite sure what kind of haze.

When they reached Mme. Blok's house he said good-bye with an absent-minded air, stammered to refuse the cup of tea Diane invited him upstairs to have. She felt him so far away that all color drained out of her cheeks. A sad, gray tide came up to submerge her. A day was over. Pierre stood motionless and silent on the edge of the sidewalk, like a criminal who wishes to become a naturalized citizen of a foreign country; and she, too conscious not to be aware that the slightest phrase would be a blunder, too close to weeping to hide her pain and just leave, brutally, without a word. A lump in her throat, haltingly: "See you, Pierre." "See you, Diane," is intoned in reply, so dismally and with such weight on each syllable that she is scarcely even surprised at the immobility of a hand that ought to be reaching out to hers. Pierre's fingers have become sadly anonymous to Diane. She believes them forever deprived of that warmth she loved so much when his fingers touched her neck, and she is incapable of consoling herself or even taking an indifferent tone. She chokes out, "See you, Pierre. I'll phone tomorrow early."

She will phone tomorrow early. Because she is walking away with a firm stride, Pierre tries to tell himself she is neither sad nor angry. He cannot, however, fail to notice that a sketch book is trembling at the end of an arm, and he can no longer banish the memory of a whole mass of sobs that is at this very instant ballooning out of that trite sentence, "See you, Pierre; I'll phone tomorrow early." Alone in the street, incapable of knowing where he is going or wants to go, he is forced to reproach himself for that trancelike state of indifference to anything that is not a fine leg, slim hips, perfect torso, an indifference into which he has fallen by the fault (should he say the "fault" or the "grace"?) of his neighbor at drawing class.

And so his eyes are sealed, and ears closed, but rather than admit to himself that he was simply aroused, sexually excited, he would prefer to blame some spell and imagine himself a victim of an evil eye. Even if he feels no compunction about having forgotten the model, that bloated, fat-faced woman on a stage, how could he not rebuke himself for having consented to be disturbed, not by a total and mysterious being, but by mere parts of a trite individual?

But although this trite individual tempts him to something far short of any quintessential ecstasy, Pierre has already on account of him exhibited indifference if not contempt toward Diane. To be sure, he did make a brief effort to recover self-control, but even if he tried with all his might the girl would still believe he was in love with her, it was all that he could do to manage a lame semblance of such feelings. He repeated a name, "Diane, Diane, Diane," and his arm tried to squeeze the arm of the person thus addressed in a more pressing, more loving way. In vain. Gentle, protective, impulses shoot out of her elbow, but none find the mark. From shoulder to wrist, his muscles have gone slack. The sleeve of a man's overcoat floated atop a woman's topcoat sleeve, and Pierre's eyes soon believed there was no longer anybody inside of either one, that neither even encased so much as a length of skeleton but only indifferent sticks. And because, despite her presence and his determination not to lose one iota of that presence, he had the unmistakable feeling that he was forgetting the best and most devoted of friends, his only friend in fact, he accuses a fate of which he has not been the master.

But already it occurs to him, by way of an excuse, that if he is not the master of his own fate, he can do no more for Diane's happiness than for his own. Therefore, he is not responsible. But, quickly, a fresh about-face. He is ashamed of his own cowardice, and lectures himself: "So you're not a man after all, Pierre?" He decides that in the future his honesty will no longer allow itself to be restricted in thoughts, words, or deeds by any weakness, even (and especially) of the emotional variety. Thus, no more feeling sorry for Diane, no more arm-squeezing, no more little walks to her door if he feels like going someplace else. And he will fear neither brutality nor cynicism. He will have the courage of his own tastes. Resolved: the courage of one's tastes. Exactly. That means the next time he will let the girl go home by herself and, instead of dodging her overprecise questions with answers on the model of "The child Septentrion danced two days and pleased" or other similar eyewash, he shall tell her straight out that if he wasn't looking where he ought to have been and if he has made up his mind not to hear a word of what she's saying, the reason is quite simply that for the moment he isn't the slightest bit concerned about all the Dianes on earth but is taken up exclusively with lusting after a certain young boy whose body deserves being followed to the ends of the earth; and in the meantime he will endeavor to find out what café that boy hangs out at, and so, obviously, he is leaving Diane, her virtue, and her sketch book on the sidewalk which she has only to follow in order to go home to her dear mother Madame Blok whom she had better stay in with from now on, anyway, instead of running around to art classes and parties to which she is drawn neither by a love for painting nor a taste for dancing but quite simply by an urge to keep Pierre from having the adventures that he is fated to have.

DIFFICULT DEATH

In such fashion, the same Diane he was a minute earlier berating himself for having mistreated suddenly becomes the accused. Will it always be the same story, affection as long as he needs her, and indifference, unjust contempt, the second she is no longer necessary?

For the moment he thinks himself above reproach and blames only the girl who he thinks is angling to marry him, and if he goes places where he hopes to run into that young man with the fine legs, slim hips, and perfect torso, it is less (he has reached the point of telling himself) to satisfy a desire about which he hardly gives a damn than to get even with Diane for making him feel guilty by her very presence, and for coming within a hair's breadth of forever preventing him from living his life.

And so it came about that Pierre found his neighbor from drawing class. Now he thinks chance has arranged things neatly in his favor, for they say his neighbor at art school is no mere would-be painter but a young composer who has just come out with a ballet score. Pierre has not been to the ballet in question, but he has already heard of the composer, Arthur Bruggle.

Arthur Bruggle. An aura of mystery shimmers around the name, which only a few months ago was unknown. All kinds of things are being said about him, and, in fact, the truth is quite interesting.

Bruggle came from America as a dishwasher on board a trans-Atlantic steamer. When he stepped ashore at Le Havre he didn't have money enough to buy a third-class train ticket to Paris. Later he was a washout as a piano player in a fourth-rate music hall. To American sailors, though, Negroes who came in to burn up the night with a last shot of booze, he brought back certain rhythms, bouquets gathered in an earlier, more savage life. At such times his eyes suddenly filled with light, as a whole ocean came to life between his opening eyelids; his nostrils flared to the smell of his own breath and lips reeking of alcohol as naturally as a fragrant flower smells of itself. Arthur was like a medium who from a substance as unfeeling as the waxed oak of the nearest table managed to conjure the mysteries of Time, and with every note he played, Arthur's hands seemed to be growing longer and thinner, so long and so thin that it was no longer even possible to imagine them (they were more like lianas in some rainforest than hands) mastering a keyboard and interweaving rhythms as subtly as any climbing vine, so that one could no longer conceive of them as an extension of a simple human creature, and Arthur himself forgot both past and present for a sightless, speechless dream.

It was on one of those nights when his fingers lengthened like an insect's antennæ to perceive the mystery of Being that he was discovered by an impressario, a manager of a dance hall who brought him to Paris to lead the establishment's jazz band. But this man exasperated him. Monsieur Arthur "had his dignity." He hadn't crossed the ocean to provide snobs of the Old and New Worlds with one more Paris-by-night distraction. As soon as he had saved a few hundred-franc notes, he flew the coop and, once at liberty, lit down in a little *pension* next door to the Jardin des Plantes. In his trunk are a tuxedo, three silk shirts, several cheap suits, a book by Ruskin, some reproductions of Quattrocento painters. On his table he has placed the photograph of a Negress whom he knew in Chicago, whose teeth, childlike eyes, and nostalgic voice he was in love with. Back in America the affair with the Negress had cost him his best friends at school in Chicago. He thinks France is the ideal country, the land of liberty, because one can have the photograph of a colored woman in one's room. He buys treatises on harmony. He spends his days, all day every day, working his way through them. Nights he goes out walking in the Paris he dreams of conquering. He walks in the rain, both hands in the pockets of a raglan overcoat that is no longer quite waterproof. He has discovered the Seine and its quais, learned that leeks are called "poor folks' asparagus," and that in certain bistros when you want a bottle of wine you call for a "kilo of white." He has read *Night in the Luxembourg* by Rémy de Gourmont and encountered the ridiculous and charming little street railway that runs down the boulevard Saint-Michel and crosses over to the Halles Centrales, where the vegetables are prettier than flowers. He combed the streets of Montmartre but was too poor to get into any of the bars, whose jazz bands seemed to him from the side-

DIFFICULT DEATH

walk considerably inferior to New York's anyway. He is often cold. He comes close to weeping. A little more of this and he would go back and play the piano in that detestable nightclub. But he braces himself, mentally repeating that he is destined to become one of the Kings of Paris, a gilded youth, and that if he plays it right and makes no mistakes he can turn every detail about himself, including his ridiculous given name of Arthur, into a seductive new wrinkle.

In the one-man deliberations which he holds each evening in his room, he passes judgment on himself as if he were a stranger named Monsieur Arthur. Monsieur Arthur would have danced for joy the first time the chambermaid in the *pension de famille* pronounced his name, which she had read out of an automatic personal curiosity, in the register that each new guest must sign.

Well, Monsieur Arthur told himself a hundred times, a thousand times over, those rainy Paris nights, that he would keep a stiff upper lip, avoid colds, and work.

He did keep a stiff upper lip, he did not catch a cold, and he did work.

He had just dipped into his last one-hundred franc note when by a miracle he chanced to get acquainted with a Rumanian woman who in twenty years had changed her name, religion, and nationality five times. When they met she was the wife of a Scandinavian diplomat and in this capacity belonged to the committee of honor of the Danish Ballet. She knew that Arthur composed, invited him to her house, asked him to tell her the story of his life. Arthur played the whole thing by ear and succeeded admirably, so much so that he had no sooner finished his story and not even yet touched the keyboard when, full of admiration for this boy who was half her age and had already chalked up three times as many adventures as she, the Rumano-Scandinavian lady promised to introduce him to the director of the Danish Ballet. She was as good as her word. Arthur was set to collaborating with a painter and a poet; a month later, the trio had hatched a ballet which enjoyed a very honorable success toward the end of that same season.

Arthur Bruggle was, if not yet famous, at least well launched.

67

RENE CREVEL

But neither the painter nor the poet (who were both pros in their respective genres) had anything outside their art and artistic ambitions to recommend them to Arthur's interest. Also (and especially) Bruggle reproached both of them for being horribly ugly. As for the Rumano-Scandinavian – although she passed for top-drawer material in the adventuress line and was rumored to have led a tumultuously wild life – Arthur failed to see what was so colorful about her. As a matter of fact, having achieved an unhoped-for degree of success and become all-powerful in the Paris of theaters and newspapers ever since her Nordic diplomat, she had assumed an unwonted air of reserve, for she still dreamed of conquering the remains of Faubourg Saint-Germain society, where she had been accepted at first out of curiosity and then regularly invited because she was amusing.

And so, because she had no particular talent that qualified her to be treated as an artist (which would not in any case have contented her since her most recent marriage), and because, moreover, she was unwilling that her role should be merely to entertain or organize parties, in order to appear as a grande dame (after having tried various means, some of which might doubtless without unfairness have been called scams), she had decided that her best strategy would be to pretend to take interest in nothing but trivia, snippets, bits-and-pieces, and to treat with levity – which she feigned but fervently believed to be a sign of true aristocracy – everything she had formerly taken seriously and for which she had expended all the resources of an extremely sophisticated political intelligence.

Thus, she went to exhausting lengths to consummate Bruggle's success, in order to derive the greatest glory for herself; but when people congratulated her on having discovered a talented young composer, she replied that his talent was considerably less seductive to her than his good looks and the charming blunders of his accent. And so it was that Arthur's vogue, which she had obtained at the price of so much campaigning and so many scheming letters, which she would have let herself be cut up in little pieces rather than acknowledge, would seem to have resulted from one of those whims of which, until her own success, she had imagined only the most aristocratic persons capable. Besides, for some time already, systematically and whether to praise or to blame, when she had to give her opinion, even (and above all) if it concerned something or someone of importance to herself, she had adopted a tone of persiflage, a certain impertinent liberty, which allowed her to seem to take no particular interest in the persons or objects proposed to her attention, and thus to be equal to the elevation of her rank. Hence her air of boredom, for example, when attending events that she had taken the trouble (and by no means small trouble) to organize, hence the distant expression that so subtly disguised her most ambitious efforts and conferred on her a sort of retroactive birthright that avenged her on all those men and women who had previously tolerated her merely because she was amusing.

She triumphed in her choice of frivolous adjectives, words normally reserved for a favorite Pekingese but which she suddenly used to describe a man for whom she felt deep admiration. Her manner, which was so familiar with anyone considered to have genius or at the very least, talent, forced one to conclude that this woman whom no one liked or respected was on a footing of virtual equality with those minds who were judged to be the best, the sharpest, and most vigorous of the age.

Thus, never abandoning such a successful tactic, and merely with a view to basking in the glory of a young protégé's success, the Rumano-Scandinavian, who would have gladly surrendered whole cascades of pearls in exchange for a simple title of nobility, which she could have pretended to have inherited from a grandmother, dragged Monsieur Arthur to houses where he could never have hoped to go, when from his America he attempted to imagine Paris, its miracles and its upper crust, on the strength of`
what he read in magazines.

To tell the truth, it infuriated him to hear his smile praised at the expense of his music, and it also alarmed him to be as boxed in, as he was, by the overprotective attentions of his discoverer. Hadn't he repeated to himself every night back in his *pension* next to the Jardin des Plantes, "Monsieur Arthur will be a gilded youth, but Monsieur Arthur will always remember that he aspires to be a great artist."

Then, too, the Rumano-Scandinavian had a way of shaking promises at him like a bunch of keys; he was beginning to feel like a prisoner. It is to be noted, moreover, that she kept him under constant surveillance and stayed at his heels as if she feared he might get lost.

He was left hardly any means of distracting himself. He had indeed tried a liaison with the first dancer that came along, for whom, if the truth be told, he had never felt a very powerful attraction, but clever publicity and the ridiculously desperate passion with which an old duke and a fat Peruvian dowager entered upon a frenzied tug-of-war over the boy before Arthur's inexperienced eyes lent him a certain glory of which Arthur would have liked to be more certain. But after a few dinners and evenings in Montmartre, Arthur judged the dancer so definitively stupid that from that time on he could no longer even tolerate his presence.

Bruggle was bored, and that is why, when he was able to escape from the Rumano-Scandinavian (whom he now called his tamer) he took refuge in the art school where Pierre Dumont and Diane Blok went to drawing class.

And it was there that Bruggle had noticed Pierre, even before Pierre noticed Bruggle. But the latter, convinced that his brand-new glory conferred on him a dignity of which he must not fall short, would not for anything in the world have been the first to make advances. He awaited Pierre's. He would willingly have hypnotized him into making them.

And so, when Pierre, after having walked Diane to her door, retraced his steps and explored the various cafés of Montparnasse until he finally found the stranger who had sat next to him in drawing class, when he found out who the stranger was, sat down, and as if accidentally brushed the hands of this person to whom he had only a short time earlier sacrificed Diane, Bruggle, happy to feel in the boy's every gesture a timid confession, at last deigned to dispense with his glory and the obstacles which Pierre's timidity, if left to its own devices, would most certainly never have overcome.

An hour later, Pierre telephoned to say he would not be back for dinner. He had scarcely hung up when he felt teeth nibbling on one of his ears, while fingers of plantlike coolness tightened round his mouth, preventing the slightest outcry, whereupon a peal of laughter rang out in response to the shock he was being prevented from expressing – Bruggle! A few moments later, facing the American, Pierre wanted to escape from his gaze, but being held by both wrists he had to submit to the hypnotic will in Bruggle's eyes. Eyes that looked like an animal's eyes. Why did Pierre still imagine he could read RATAPOILOPOLIS written on the wall? Ratapoilopolis, insanity. A cloud passed over Bruggle's eyes, and he was afraid without being aware of Pierre's fear. Slowly, the vicelike grip relaxed. Hands pressed against hands, palms wedded palms. Pierre shuddered and then was nothing but a droplet of blood transfused into another life's bloodstream.

Incapable of pulling himself together in his own skin, in his body which he no longer even remembered, Pierre accepted Bruggle's whole face, that mask of skin that already touched his cheek.

Bruggle's face, a mask of skin. It was cold. Pierre saw no more of it than an eye; as for himself, little by little he altogether ceased to exist.

Needless to say, Diane hated the composer at first sight. But the jealousy she inevitably felt as soon as Pierre told her of his new friend (and that was the next day) instead of provoking anger or reproachful thoughts only made her feel sorrier for him. The overwet kisses, the studied slips and allusions to her fictitious private life and tastes all dated from that moment. She intended them to put her on the same level as Pierre, just as some women, ashamed of the sinful life they lead, feel obliged to prevaricate and put on a semblance of virtue in the hope of once more becoming, or at least seeming, worthy of the man they love; Diane, in hopes that remorse would not alienate Pierre from the innocent young girl she thought he considered her and that he would not be continually exposed to fresh reasons for lowering his estimate of himself, took steps to enable him to suspect her along the same lines.

But as words have wings (Diane had been to first-year law school and was familiar with the adage, *Verba volant, scripta manent*), she took the opportunity while on a trip to write Pierre that she had had lovers. She had decided that in this manner she would be better defended against herself and would never again be tempted to blame Pierre for anything whatever.

And so Diane puts up with Bruggle, as she would have put up with anyone or anything, in order not to lose Pierre. But even though Pierre realizes that she has made great sacrifices in his behalf and is ready and willing to make even more, he is seldom willing to admit to himself how selfish he really is. He is even capable, for example, of accepting the idea that he is a victim and that, torn between Arthur and Diane, he suffers from never having been able to distinguish love from friendship. A fine excuse, which even its author, who invented it for his own convenience, finds difficult to put over on himself. In fact, Pierre goes back to Diane only when Bruggle refuses to see him, but, incapable of liberating himself from his need for the American, on evenings when he is deprived of him, after having been with Diane at the theater or alone, eating his heart out, he was at last reduced to the attempt, aided by the most vile partners, to recapture an illusion after which he hungered and thirsted with all his soul. As he sought to merge his being by a sort of sensual proxy with another being – not the one he was actually touching, but the other, true, absent one – his mind comes to hate that other mind which he will never truly know, and which, nonetheless, he would like to think the tangible and sentient kernel of the succulent human body enclosing it. And so he contents himself with the most sordid adventures and is at times so thoroughly disgusted that he likes to see himself as an object of self-inflicted punishment. But to onlookers, he is like nothing so much as a small animal in heat. "Pierre is like a dog," Bruggle exclaims.

Pierre is like a dog. Angrily, he repeats the insult to himself. Insult added to injury. To be called a dog, when all this feverish sex comes from anxiety and he considers himself a victim, assuring himself that if his mother had not inspired in him through her attitude a contempt for the so-called fair sex he might have been the most carefree and happy of ladies' men. He is well aware that for Arthur love will never lose its playful joyousness and æsthetic self-assurance. The young American loves to make a theatrical production out of pyjamas, surprising underpants, clever sheets. Arthur has too great a taste for objects to be sensitive to what Pierre calls (not without pride and for a bitter compensation whose vanity he would prefer not to see) the basic problems.

That handsome animal Arthur has always seemed as supple and well-made in mind as in body, but Pierre knows he will never understand statements like the following, which he cannot help repeating even though it flagrantly contradicts his insatiable appetite for Bruggle: "Those who have truly obsessed me have always done so as psychic presences, not bodies." Likewise the urge to know each other intimately, which Bruggle senses in Pierre, appalls the American, and he readily exclaims, "You and Diane have a common fault, which is that both of you are much too introspective."

Arthur is doubtless quite right. After all, he is happy, knows how to use people and things, would turn into a fish if he fell in the sea, and never loses his weapon, a flirtatiousness whose artless whims often lend him that joy in seduction which gives all its beauty to a face whose eyes were the first thing one noticed, if only, it seemed, to forget an implausible first impression of innocence in favor of the seagreen satanism of their habitual look.

This is why people who had never allowed themselves to be taken in by Bruggle and his games would never understand the irresistible spell cast on others by this New Yorker – his Rumano-Scandinavian "tamer" was doubtless quite right to prefer his good looks and grace to the ballet score, which was the pretext but not the true cause of his success. The power that is Bruggle's has nothing to do with intelligence in the European sense of the word. Come up out of the depths of his being, Arthur's is a potency transcending all means of conscious self-expression, and it would be both unjust and inexact to speak of cunning with regard to him; but a mysterious energy bursts out of him like electricity from a cat's fur. A feline floating in a baggy jacket, a feline with big shoes ("The French," he says, "love shoes, not feet, clothes but not bodies, and that's why they live in such narrow, velvet-and-leather-lined rooms!"), Arthur, lost in his raglan overcoat, with each of his gestures puts one in mind not so much of all the hard work and study implicit in the elasticity of his movements as of the very instincts that predetermined the nature and direction of that study. Watching him walk, Pierre often said to himself that the cruel, savage possibilities always remain identical to themselves in a panther's dance.

Diane prefers dogs to cats (even if she were not caught up in this jealousy towards Bruggle, which she moreover feels too specifically to suffer in all of its effects), and so Diane comes naturally by her aversion to Bruggle. Understanding as she is, and wishing more than anything in the world to free Pierre from the phantoms of Ratapoilopolis whose howling legions Mme. Dumont-Dufour daily hurls against him, Diane cannot bear to see Arthur, so full of himself and endowed with a coquetry at once too subtle and too demanding not to be of an at least relative chastity, treating Pierre with contempt because the fear of insomnia and being alone in the dark forces him into adventures from which he derives more remorse or disgust than pleasure.

She knows, and suffers from knowing, that he will never find a safe haven in the cool arms of a woman; and to excuse and perhaps also not to go sour on the sisterly role with which she will have to content herself, she recalls that Pierre is the first to say he is unhappy with the life he leads and is inflicting upon her, and she thinks that if he had not been deprived of that robust healthiness that has made it possible for her to endure without any definitive emotional reaction Mme. Blok's monologues on M. Blok's suicide, Pierre would not go out – as he puts it – "cruising."

Cruising. For he has no idea where he is going, once he is no longer mute and motionless in an armchair undergoing the most excruciating tortures beneath the gaze of Mme. Dumont-Dufour, implacable in her thirst for vengeance.

Mme. Dumont-Dufour's thirst for vengeance.

Pierre is weary.

He feels that all the strength he has will be drained out of him in this duel.

Why has he never had the courage to get out? If he were only self-sufficient. But he needs others, and Arthur is no refuge. As for Diane, hasn't he already repeated at least a hundred times in the past hour that he wouldn't be capable of living with her?

In that case, who?

No one.

Pierre has a headache. Night has fallen. Mme. Dumont-Dufour turns on the light and asks in a dry voice, "Well?"

Pierre makes no reply. It is called to his attention that he has had ample time to reflect:

"Speak!"

"Of what?"

A pair of shoulders shrugs beneath Moroccan silk:

"Are you going to talk?"

"I have nothing to tell you."

"You have nothing to tell me. Are you quite sure about that?"

An ascending musical scale of derisive laughter follows. Mme. Dumont-Dufour wishes to get on to the main scene without further ado, so she tries to think of a line guaranteed to bring down the house. Failing this, she chokes with rage and finally skewers him with:

"You miserable little abortion!"

Pierre: "All right, I am a poor specimen, but whose fault is that? Please be assured that, if I had made you, you would have been even more charmingly proportioned than you already are."

"Abortion!" Mme. Dumont-Dufour repeats. "And one," she goes on to explain, "that was no fault of my own but your father's, that father you respect and admire so much, whereas I, who have done everything in the world for you and sacrificed myself..."

RENE CREVEL

Pierre can see the whole thing coming – both the monologue and the army of nightmares. He will not put up with either one. Let Mme. Dumont-Dufour show what a skillful, tricky opponent she can be – Pierre will counter with power, even brutality. He grabs her by both scrawny wrists, whose bones his fingers take pleasure in squeezing a bit too hard, then says, without violence, but firmly:

"I forbid you to mention 'Ratapoilopolis' or Colonel Dumont."

A shriek of laughter. Mme. Dumont-Dufour extricates herself but Pierre gives her no time to work up new rhetorical effects:

"Shut up. I forbid you to complain. You have no right to complain. If your husband hadn't gone insane, you wouldn't have a thing to talk about with all your friends and old bags like Madame Blok."

Mme. Blok an "old bag"? If Pierre were only willing to be polite. Doesn't he owe some consideration to his mother and his mother's friends?

Pierre thinks Ratapoilopolis will definitely be back on the agenda within moments. He gets up.

"Good-bye."

"You're not staying for dinner?"

"No. I'm leaving this house."

"What?"

"I'm getting out, leaving."

"But you don't have any money to your name!"

"Bruggle sold one of my paintings to the wife of a Scandinavian diplomat."

"Ah, now I understand. His nibs wishes to live his life. Your friend Bruggle…"

"Good-bye."

The door slams. A sound of feet galloping down the stairs. Pierre is already in the street. Mme. Dumont-Dufour shrugs her shoulders and rings for the maid to come and remove the scraps and accessories left over from tea.

Chapter Three
DINNER with DIANE

Once in the street, Pierre's first thoughts are of Bruggle. So are his first steps, which lead him straight to the telephone booth in the nearest café. The metal part of the receiver fogs over when picked up, revealing the fever in his hands. His voice slurs, wavers, burns. It burns with the kind of fire that parches the mouths of men in whose prayers the repetition of a chosen divinity's name turns into a lugubrious earthbound echo. Pierre pronounces the name of a famous battle (or rather, that of a telephone exchange commemorating the battle) followed by the numbers that enable him to reach the man on whom he has pinned all his hopes. As he speaks, his mother's threats keep hissing in his ears. *Ratapoilopolis.* By himself he will never be capable of routing that army of phantoms with plaster-cast eyes and lipless smiles. He has attempted to retreat, but even now, from an Auteuil apartment his movements are being monitored by a Marlborough in petticoat-breeches, driven on by menopause, a mania for war-games in the home, and the need to taste final vengeance. Even now, alone in her dining room, sitting straight as a ramrod, and holding her spoon in the haughtiest fashion, Mme. Dumont-Dufour must be bolting her soup in two swallows with the indifference of a Spartan warrior over his gruel; for, exactly like a Spartan, the daughter of Justice Dufour, ever since she began to breathe, eat, drink, talk, walk (and also from the time she started surrendering herself, a martyred spouse, to the Colonel every Saturday night) has always been oblivious to the pleasures one can take from the actions of everyday life and has never forgotten that there was an enemy to be pursued and crushed (although at times she was not altogether clear as to the enemy's identity). After a quick meal she will polish up her hatpins and sally forth in full battle array, in quest of allies. Pierre is aware that she will encircle Mme. Blok, attempt to cast a spell on Diane, and confer with the Bloks' cousin Bricoulet, that specialist and amateur of catastrophes.

Hence Pierre's need for shelter. He is calling Bruggle, whose wonder-working presence is bound to do the trick, if anything ever will. A telephone number, an open sesame to happiness, the breath bearing those magic syllables is a flame, and after it has passed into the mouthpiece, Pierre's lips, as if by the effect of two opposite weights, fall into each other as weakly as the petals of a flower killed by the sun. An aquarium of anxiety, this shadow-box Pierre has shut himself up in is not yet warm with the voice of his beloved, gentler than a gracefully curvaceous Gulf Stream. Phone receivers cling to ears, avid as octopi. Behind the curtain of the eyelids is no night, but a mauve sea, some of whose stacked waves must recede, the swimmer of silence cannot tell which. Blue, color of hope; red, color of rage. Undersea joys and algæ of doubt brush past, only aggravating his impatience to where, Pierre thinks, a man of Moses' stamp, nay Moses himself would have gone out of his mind had the thunderclap on Mount Sinai repeated itself too many times before splitting apart like a properly reasonable fruit, that cloud out of which God the Father came forth with the Tables of the Law.

Suddenly he hears the jingling that must be the operator's signal. Pierre has no wish to contain his joy. Fervently he repeats the syllables that will allow him to reach and hear his savior. Reach, hear, communicate, commune. He will speak and be spoken to. His sentences will lead, Arthur will follow. Their voices will be reciprocal magnets. Their voices will be tightrope dancers and acrobats whose transparent hearts and hands of light will lift and unite them in a sunburst of joy.

Pierre wouldn't have had the courage to go directly to Bruggle's house without first calling. "Your friend Bruggle," his mother had said in the tone she might have used to say, "Your idol." His

DIFFICULT DEATH

Bruggle, yes. His idol, no. Bruggle was his God. And Pierre did not ever presume himself to be a creature in that God's image. He always seeks the other's consent, as if it were a required visa, but without granting himself any reciprocal rights. And so, for example, he would never under any circumstances dare go to Arthur's place without first having been invited. He thus rejoices in the trammels and curtailments of submission and, as he repeats the name of a battle followed by numbers, congratulates himself for fearing Bruggle and fearing him sufficiently not to have been tempted to make a trip that would in any case have seemed unbearably long. And he not only throws himself on the mercy of the man but on the mercy of anything (persons or objects) that could bring him closer to that man. For instance, he just tried to sweet talk the phone operator. Note, however, that the latter chose to react as if he were joking, and saw nothing but a joke in Pierre's blend of submissiveness and zeal – like that of a true believer not altogether sure of himself and therefore obliged to have recourse to saints and other blessed intermediaries. In reply he got a snicker – merely a drop or two of icewater to his fever. He opened his eyes then in hopes of seeing something that would make him feel better but at first found nothing in the darkness of the little booth in which the light was not turned on; but having gotten used to the dark, his attention was suddenly drawn to a piece of dirty cardboard that was scored and scribbled over in a way that made a coincidental drawing of Diane's face. Diane's face. The face he saw on days when he was relatively calm thanks to her tenderness. On such days Pierre let Diane guess that to him she was no more on the whole than a household remedy, and, not having enough energy for the simplest courtesy, instead of letting her stay, as soon as he no longer needed her, despite her wish to linger just a few more minutes, he did his best to make her leave and, had she been too slow to take the hint, would have thrown her out with a harsh word. Thus, in a year of knowing her, Pierre has given Diane less consideration than he has shown a recalcitrant telephone operator in five minutes.

Just as he condemns the way in which he has been taking ad-

RENE CREVEL

vantage of Diane and her kindness, he judges unpardonable the sweetness and light he has been dispensing in order to make a faster telephone connection; and like one whose prayers have not moved his heavenly intercessors and who accuses a God he has never before spoken to directly, either because he could not or did not dare, now suddenly he laughs at his superstition and feels himself ready to renounce Bruggle altogether. The need and the fear he continues to feel, thinking of Bruggle, excite him to blasphemy; and, no doubt, his thirst for revenge is by no means so strong as his belief that a sin against Bruggle, be it merely a sinful thought, will earn him a punishment at the hands of one who already weighs too heavy on his soul. Actual physical torture is the only thing commensurate with his passion and – suffering at the mute God's hands for having wished him dead – Pierre will be lashed every minute with the god's silence so cruelly that his empty ears will fill with a song that no one else can ever hear.

The tide has yet to come in that will sweep him away to the isles of the silent blessed. Pierre is now a prisoner, left to the tender mercies of a telephone operator. A jumble of scribbles, unintelligible in themselves, make him more than ever acutely aware of a certain sadness not his own, but concerning which it is only fair that he should suffer. Diane, whom he had intended to drown in the deepest oblivion, has bobbed back to the surface. Because he lacked the courage to take the burden of responsibility for his ingratitude upon himself, he blames Bruggle's bad influence. Completely engrossed in Arthur, tirelessly seeking even in his silences or his sometimes uncouth laughter fresh reasons to admire him, how could he not at length discern his exaggerated humility? And not only has he failed to appreciate the blessing Diane represents as anything better than an herbal remedy to help him get to sleep when tormented by insomnia, but, on top of that, he has never tried to stop the poor girl from making the declarations, insinuations, and false slips concerning herself that she was inventing out of whole cloth because she thought them proper to put her on the same (if not a lower) plane with a certain boy she loves too much to accept his becoming an object of self-contempt. Now,

DIFFICULT DEATH

today, he realizes that likewise he has made himself smaller both in Bruggle's eyes and in his own, and less, no doubt, out of humility than in order to give the beloved what he has thought to be the ultimate gift: one's self-respect.

From a telephone booth where impatience multiplies the power of memories, Pierre remembers that he has always been ashamed. Ashamed of his face, irregular and chaotic as it is, in which (he thinks) only the look in his eyes exhibits a sporadic but unquestionable glimmering of intelligence. Ashamed, too, of his body and, what is worse, ashamed of the compliments and desires his body has given rise to (for instance, the boxer's "You're a strange little bird"). Ashamed of the way he moves, especially during sex, the need for which possesses him only the better to ensure the triumph of disgust over his own depraved flesh. Ashamed of his thoughts – the essential part of him, no doubt – being powerless against their surprises; and resolutions to turn over a new leaf (which he has always in all objectivity judged best) remain impotent when such thoughts hold sway over him.

This shame could (Pierre reminds himself) prevent anyone at all, including even Bruggle, in whom he strains to discover perfection, from enjoying the slightest feelings of justifiable pride or self-respect. Only that comparison which each of us essays between his own life and the lives of others allows us to judge ourselves with relative indulgence; even then, we fail to grasp the overall personality, whose elements, by an incurable tendency to mimicry, transform themselves at each new encounter beyond all possibility in fact of unraveling anything other than an interweave of reflex actions. This is why, in a pair of friends or a couple, the one who feels heightened, expansive (and is in fact growing) will always, whether consciously or not, attempt to lower himself in the other's eyes. Thus Pierre underestimates himself the better to admire Bruggle. Were the truth but known, were he but capable of judging his friend by a pattern other than himself, he would have some notion of the qualities peculiar to Bruggle over which he could so easily have powers like those of a sorcerer. Pierre has no sense of his limits and therefore doubts his own existence;

81

RENE CREVEL

Pierre has no clear perception of any of his instincts or spontaneous tastes – not that these are by any means lacking in him, but because they all seethe in the very depths of his being, while he often imagines himself lost in other souls, and only a singular peninsula allows him to declare his independence of the universal and anonymous continent; however, it is never easy to become a mirror, and he has consistently refused everything of Bruggle's that might have enriched his life, and has not learned from Bruggle to enjoy flashy neckties, long, wide shoes, the objects and the acts that demonstrate to a man his own power and potency, and the act of love. Bruggle may dominate Pierre, but he has not relieved him of the old obsessions. A slave of himself even in the hour of his imagined self-surrender, Pierre obviously lacks the antennæ or other sensory apparatus by means of which he might understand the kind of happiness and dignity this boy savage Bruggle hopes to find under the sun. The most self-centered of women will always succeed better at forgetting themselves than the most detached of men. Pierre, who is sincerely convinced of his own humility and for Bruggle's sake would have been willing to turn himself inside out like a glove, never actually sought in Bruggle anything other than a perfection identical to that which would be Pierre's if he were any good at living. Yet the traits common to both Pierre and Bruggle seem to exist only the better to highlight all of the many ways in which they differ.

Diane, on the other hand, has never attempted to see any similarity whatever between herself and Pierre; yet she – not through coquettish calculation, but spontaneously – has become parallel to the one she loves. Thus it happens that she has grown on Pierre to the point where a shapeless scrawl on the wall of a phone booth comes alive for him. The apparition nourishes feelings of remorse, and hands that were only just now burning go ice-cold. The metal handle becomes their brother, as around Diane's head there gathers a halo consisting of everyone Pierre has ever known, cut up in pieces. A chaos of memory. Foreign lands, outdoors, at the theater – Pierre has never been able to keep them sorted out – and his feelings of shame increase by leaps and bounds. Out in

DIFFICULT DEATH

the street he was cold but his heart needed warm clothes, too, begged of every passing stranger, for which he got nothing but rags, and so went shivering in a fool's motley like a masquerader dragging home at dawn when the dance hall shuts and snow falls over gaudy posters. He had wanted to think things over, get organized, but it all slipped through his fingers and there isn't a grain of sense left in him. Only the Colonel, Mme. Dumont-Dufour, Diane, Bruggle, and a host of others. In all these and not in himself he sought to discern coming joys and torments. He is therefore so illogical that, judging Bruggle alongside himself, he must now admit he has never stopped expecting others to make his dreams come true. Armed by self-exasperation, he runs himself down to the extent of seeing in his most dreadful depressions (how nice it would be to blame them on some metaphysical anguish) the simple mark of a sullen mind, inherited from Mme. Dumont-Dufour whose bickering disposition feeds on every domestic hap and mishap down to the most trivial and finds in each a taste of ashes.

Further, because of his mother, who in order to excite his sympathy and also to lower his opinion of the Colonel, told him the story of her wedding night and spared no details, from the bitten shoulder to the maidenhead ravished by a man who had not even taken the time to pull his boots off (though the Colonel had passed himself off as a well-bred person and a gentleman), Pierre, each time his mouth wanders over a body whose flesh tempts his teeth, or in the urgency of his desire flings himself, still half-clad, on an arm, a chest, a leg, or a belly, once his frenzy is appeased, imagines that after such acts he is purely and simply doomed to Ratapoilopolis.

The strength of a Bruggle, to the contrary, lies in that he fits inside his ego as naturally as an orange in its rind; never uncomplicated but always harmonious. His easygoing nature prompted Pierre to exclaim one day when they first knew each other, "Seeing this boy feels exactly like taking a good hot bath!" It is a pity he does not always recall this judgment. Then, instead of straining to find similarities between himself and his beloved, he would simply congratulate himself on having met a man capable of turning into a bird if he took it into his head to fly. In this fashion he would never have needed to be so rough on himself so that Bruggle could triumph.

To be sure, in the sacrifices which on the one hand Pierre grants Bruggle and on the other Diane grants Pierre, adoring humility is not the sole deciding factor; there is also an element of calculation, thanks to which the most fervent self-immolator will rejoice more and better in whatever favor is accorded him. The sorrier the beggar, the more handsome the alms. One day, alas, this beggar – who still had a long road ahead of him down which to stagger, drunk with wretchedness, reduced to slavery – will have to admit that the only thing that constrains him to accept a sad fate and persist in the will to live is an inept dread of being abandoned forever.

For the time being, Pierre, who would not have had the patience to walk to Bruggle's house, is condemned to stamp his feet in a narrow booth where the young lady employed by the telephone administration is having fun prolonging a wait which she hopes is as feverish as it sounds. He has no illusions about the anxieties forced upon him by this submissiveness toward Bruggle, on which he was willing to congratulate himself only just now. But, though he is suffering from not having reached the number he asked for, and just as much as if the slowness in reaching that damned number depended solely on Bruggle's wishes, all of Pierre's rage turns back on himself and he says he is only a callow youth who knows a bit about how to organize a prize essay but absolutely nothing about how to get organized in real life. "Real life" – there, he's talking like his mother. Real life indeed. Given his father's insanity and the hatred aimed at him by Mme. Dumont-Dufour (didn't she reject good sense to the point of keeping him beneath her sad petticoats long enough for him to have no more than a vague notion of what he vaguely calls "real life" despite his frenzied nocturnal attempts to get closer to it?) and the fact that Bruggle does not deign to answer his call, which although it is being sent from the first available phone booth rather than from a raft of the "Raft

DIFFICULT DEATH

of the Medusa" type is nonetheless a desperate cry for help, Pierre is alone in the world. Further, as if being incarcerated in this booth were not wretched enough for him, in order to make himself ten times more upset he decrees that Diane's tenderness is definitely worth no more than a sleep-inducing tea, and...

"Hello!" growls a voice at the other end of the line.

"Finally! Hello! It's me, Pierre."

"Hi."

"I'd like to see you."

"Why?"

"First, because it would be fun. Then I have a whole bunch of things I want to ask your advice about."

At the other end of the line, Bruggle seems to be in no great hurry to be dispensing advice about a whole bunch of things. But Pierre hastens to interrupt a series of unconcerned uh-huhs:

"I walked out on my mother."

"Excellent."

"I'm glad you approve, Arthur. Would you like to have dinner with me?"

Of an elation that was shooting upwards on each syllable of the last sentence, soon there is nothing left but a wave breaking on a reef. Bruggle, in his reply, has just been colder and harder than a rock:

"Have dinner with you? Impossible."

Splashed with the foam of that sad wave, Pierre could easily imagine his hair, skin, and eyes all turned white. White as his voice:

"Really and truly, Arthur, you can't have dinner with me?" Is the supplication in these words so touching, then? For once, Pierre will challenge the established "Monsieur Arthur" system.

"I can't possibly have dinner with you, Pierre, but come by this evening. I'm having some friends over. If you can't eat by yourself, or don't feel like it, call Diane."

"Good, Arthur. Thanks, see you in a couple of hours."

Without even a moment's silence or hesitation, Pierre adds, by way of a coy (and gratuitous) lie:

"You know, Arthur, I'm speaking to you from the very same phone booth where you and I first..."

A sound of female laughter, and Pierre has no choice but to notice that he is alone on the line with the eavesdropping operator. Bruggle has hung up on him without bothering to say good-bye. But unwilling, even in his mind, to rebuke Bruggle, he is already placing another call:

"Hello. It's Pierre. Have you already sat down to dinner?"

"I was just about to."

"You wouldn't like to have dinner with me?"

"Of course I would! Where? I'll be right there."

Fifteen minutes later, Pierre and Diane arrive separately at the door of the restaurant.

"Hi, Diane."

"Hi, Pierre. You're looking out of sorts. Is anything wrong?"

Without answering, Pierre takes Diane's arm and squeezes it, this time without shamming. They go in and sit down at a table, Diane happy, amused at being called "Madame," Pierre a little light-headed with hunger and overheated from his exertions of the past hour. He looks at Diane but very soon he no longer sees her. In the telephone booth, a crude scribble on the wall had sufficed (anything at all, actually, would have worked just as well) to conjure up Diane's presence. From that instant, although absent, in her human role fated to know nothing of his anxiety or of the words that would follow it, she had been the eyewitness of Pierre's feverish wait, a telephone operator's willful slowness, and Bruggle's indifference. But now he is in fact released from all anxiety imputable to Bruggle, not seeing him but sufficiently sure of soon being in his presence not to suffer anymore, there descends between Pierre and Diane a fog out of which he knows a new Bruggle will be reborn to torture him.

Diane, Bruggle, Diane, Bruggle. The syllables get mixed up, as well as the two persons denoted by them. The smell of a meat dish no longer evokes a restaurant dining room. All of the props that make up dinner – tables, chairs, tablecloths, forks, spoons, knives, and Diane herself – become disconnected and the elements linking them vanish. Walls are removed. Pierre's eyes behold a spectacle without object. Already the other night he went the route of sleep to a point no word could name.

He was alone. He was empty. The adventure had begun when those ruby-and-felt birds, his lungs, had flown out of his petrified throat and soared up in the middle of the sky, sweeter than angels, which however as everyone knows are boneless creatures, and his chest, prouder than the hull of a brand-new ship, had rejoiced as if at last rid of a rather stupid virginity. And out there on the highway, soldiers met the empty throat, and the soldiers lifted their eyes to heaven and saw a red stain in the sun; then, their boots tramping out the beat, they sang:

Virginity, virginity
Is just a lovesick chickadee
That never gets out of her cage
Until she's fifteen years of age…

Lungs, virginity, blood-flecked birds, a lovesick chickadee. The cage stands empty; the cage stands by itself. Its prisoner has soared up to the stars. Here it comes back down, metamorphosed into a face with closed eyes, perfect features, and cheeks you immediately know are smoother than wax to the hands and lips that touch them. The eyelids are joined so perfectly that one would have thought them to be the two halves of a single shell – what invisible bite makes the eyes pop out like plum pits? Amid shadows of temples, nostrils, and chin, a sudden look bursts into flower. An uneven look, though both eyes are very much alive. And the traits of the face have completely faded out. In that solitary space, that void facing the boy with the hollow body, there remain only two eyes – one of them Bruggle's eye, the other Diane's.

Diane's eye is precise and sad. It belongs to a consciousness that puts limits on what it sees. Bruggle's eye is the handsomest human eye Pierre has ever seen. A human eye, also an animal eye that not even love could ever tame. Boy savage Bruggle's eye twinkles out of the forest primæval, dry wood, rain. One droplet of his liquid gaze is deeper than all the oceans on earth piled one on top of the other. Bruggle's eye, an animal eye. Bruggle, the boy savage. He was quite right to laugh at the Scandinavian ambassador's lady. His tamer, as he calls her, may know how to handle men, but in him she has found one she will never tame. Bruggle, the boy savage, his eye is clear and free. Diane's eye, precise, sad, and of a consciousness that limits what it sees.

The two eyes, two enemy brothers, move toward each other. Pierre at first thought there would be some kind of fight. Already they touch but the eyelashes do not quiver, and without the slightest sign of hostility, Pierre can see Bruggle's eye beneath Diane's which has become transparent. Then there is nothing at all in that solitary space, that void.

A deluge of sweet lava sweeps over the whole thing, and Pierre realizes that death is the point in space and time where all the looks, people, things, minutes, places, acts, regrets, joys, hopes, rages, cries, tears, and laughter converge in a swirl of mutual destruction. And there is nothing left but a hole that is whiter than white in whiteness, blacker than black on black.

Such big eyes, and so wide open they seemed empty; Bruggle is never so handsome as when, lost in God knows what daze, his eyes seem to sink deeper in their sockets, to the point that it is no longer believable that such mysterious cavities could be found in a human face.

But how should Pierre have the courage tonight to become a living man again, a young one at that? He eats without saying a word to his dinner partner, whereas alone, he would not even have had the courage to sit at the table. With movements light as shadows, he passes the pepper, the salt, the serving dishes.

Under the tablecloth he clasps his hands.

Will he pray for forgiveness, for not having properly appreciated the joys with which Diane wished to make his cup run over? Inwardly Pierre laughs bitterly. He no longer believes in the possibility of joy for himself. Yet his hunger for Bruggle will never subside. He has of late been spending all his time admiring Bruggle's body, which is like a tree, at once hard and supple, robust yet gracile. His body. That body and the lianas it sends out, subtle bridges fragrant with the precise scent of his gestures and the

DIFFICULT DEATH

petals of his voice and of his hands – two flowers snatched from Ophelia's crown – and of the most improbable of plants whose curves his footsteps follow in a special way of walking that could never quite help turning very rapidly into a dance.

Hunger, hunger still, and always hunger, that vigilant langorousness when, watching over the other's sleep, he lays his hand over a crucible of cool flesh, Bruggle's chest, and as soon as dawn comes through the curtains he gazes upon two slightly bulging, fruit-sweet triangles, eyelids blue from a feast of sensuality, like sun-ripened prunes. Eyelids, you are being brushed, brushed by the lips of one not asleep, with the furtive caution of a female thief, but reaching your eyelashes they suddenly take flight, fearing these portcullises that defend men's secrets and the lovely-hued résumés of their eyes. That definitive forehead in the sour uncertainty of the early-morning light, a definitive forehead in the midst of a rumpled bed, in what wood was its look of smooth contentment carved? In what wood or marble? Pierre's skull is a sad house of bone, and its roof of hair is of the most miserable thatch. Bruggle's head, on the contrary, lacquered with a cruel innocence, is the temple in which Youth imbues all things with beauty. The goddess of Youth. The sleeper is one with her and ignorant of nightmares. Bruggle is not one of those who await the evening of life, or even allow it to come. He will not die, but evaporate in the most insolent of lights like one of those clouds born at noon, which after having amused themselves at dropping, from a sky too hot and harsh, the promise of a moistened earth, at sunset no longer soften that leaden cover next to the horizon from which no one continues to hope for necklaces of rain.

But, because this freshness is not yet about to fade, and as if it were to last only to make him happy, Pierre convinces himself that Bruggle, the boy savage, is only too ready and willing to help, for him to allow himself any sadness in the foreground this evening. Dinner with Diane (this silence is not boredom) serves as a simple transition. It is the bridge between Mme. Dumont-Dufour and Bruggle, from an adolescence falsified by sadness to real youth, from lukewarm qualms to raw joys. In only a couple of hours, he

will be leaving the old terrors behind forever. The insolent innocence that will be his from this evening on will do more than a
tropical sun to change the remaining hours of his life into a golden
age.

It was only unhappiness that led him to his present dinner partner, Diane, gentle companion of his winter afternoons and sister
in the summer shade. Silently he moves away from her; he wants
to believe that Bruggle, his brother in light, will save him. The season of tenderness under gray skies and gentle rains is over. Pierre
no longer needs a nurse to take him on walks through joyless
streets. His fear of impetuous winds and angry waves will be trans-
formed, thanks to Bruggle, into that restless audacity that goes
when it decides to go and gives adventures all their zest.

From Bruggle, Pierre will derive the strength never to need anyone. From this very evening, since Bruggle invited him to come
(he has no recollection that Bruggle invited him because he felt
sorry for him), from a moment not more than an hour from now,
shall date the kingdom of joy on earth. Already Diane, whose eyes
have not left Pierre's face, is surprised by the smile that colors his
lips. She is surprised, then sad, then terrified in quick succession.
Like a mother who sees her sick child suddenly looking better,
although she has not been able to discern the slightest signs of an
improvement she has been anxiously watching for, Diane instead
of rejoicing is afraid that, no longer needing her, Pierre will stop
loving her altogether or will lose that languorous grace that
touched her heart and permitted what to her mind ought to have
been a simple friendship to blossom into love. Diane, her elbows
on the table and her chin cushioned in the palms of her hands,
knows there will be no answer to the interrogation of her silence.

Opposite but very close, a boy is moving away as steadily as if
each of his successive thoughts were an oar stroke. His air of unhappiness, which she had cherished for the many prayers and
promises it represented (and it was an air that craved the help she
was only too happy to give), has now become an absent air. Were
she to try talking, Pierre would never hear. And so, because she
thinks she will never again be able to help him in any way, she

makes no attempt to find the words that might break his silence.

Thanks to Mme. Blok who came home in a tailspin and confessed to having caused trouble with her question, "Is he abnormal?" Diane knows that a row must certainly have taken place between Pierre and his mother. Not unaware of any of Mme. Dumont-Dufour's techniques in the art of persecution, as soon as she heard Pierre's voice on the telephone she told herself he must be suffering and her presence would do him good. But now they would soon be finished with their dinner, and Pierre, she repeats to herself, has not unclenched his jaws except to say hello and eat. He persists in keeping the whole business to himself, and the girl would readily believe that he asked her to come only to treat her to the spectacle of his brand-new detachment. On other evenings already, he had complained wordlessly; on such occasions he had taken Diane's hands and laid them like a cold compress on his feverish brow; and cool fingers, tender magnets, uprooted from his skull the pains with which he was tormented. But tonight she is no longer being asked for anything, she regrets the patient's recovery, and at the same time is ashamed of herself, for she has got to admit that if she was willing to soothe Pierre's waking nightmares it was less with a view to the benefit he would derive from it than her own joy in the hours spent with him.

The palms of her hands are a pair of white swallows whose nests are Pierre's aching temples. They mustn't shiver, they mustn't burn with fever. In front of her mirror, Diane taught herself a face that looked exactly like a smile. It hurt to do it. It felt just like lifting one's lips with safety pins. But she liked to think Pierre was taken in by the falsehood of a mouth fixed in an expression of happiness. As soon as she had left him, on those days when he had been shut in with his own pain without a single affectionate word for her, Diane would let the mask drop, and a sudden mirror revealed that two tiny wrinkles were all that remained of the smile she had been counterfeiting for hours. Two tiny wrinkles. She recalled that Pierre had told her earlier that he would be spending the evening with Bruggle, and, even though she meant to forbid herself to be jealous, she thought that after dinner she would not know what to do. But, as always, she managed to repress all hateful thoughts. One night in bed, she had not been able to sleep, and to her shame had imagined another bed in which Bruggle's head lay next to Pierre's. To her further shame, she went on to imagine their bodies beneath the sheets, extensions of those two heads, one of which was the most detested and the other the most beloved in her life. At this point Diane, her fingernails digging into her hands so that the pain would tear her away from these poisonous musings, forced herself to forget others' faults and pity their sufferings. She would always remember a vow she had made that evening when her mother, petrified in her pink-and-cream satin, had shrieked, "My baby, your father is dead, he killed himself." She had seen the dead man when they cut him down and laid him on the couch, and all the guests blacker than crows, crowding round the big stiff doll he had become, in checked trousers and shirtsleeves, his tongue stuck out. When they laid him back down, his eyes closed but not in sleep, the child Diane, who believed that prayers could save a soul, her hands joined over her breast, swallowing tears that her firmly closed eyelids would not hold back, promised her brand-new plaster Jesus (she had just turned twelve) that she would always go to the wretched and unfortunate, like that woman in the Gospels who washed the Son of God's feet with her hair. Later, when the fresh plaster Jesus was no more than an image of her own childhood, even at moments when Mme. Blok with her refrain "Suicide is like carrot-heads" tempted Diane with a death wish that she thought it as natural to carry around as the name of the man whose child she was, and if, for example, she told herself that guns weren't only for stray dogs and that on certain days it was quite convenient to live in a sixth-floor apartment, there always remained in the background that wish she had made the evening she had first gotten acquainted with Death. Beliefs she no longer held still dominated her life. Thus, in the name of a Charity whose principle was much deeper rooted in her heart than in the catechism where she had first learned the theological term for it, from the day when she first met Pierre she resigned herself to being for him no more than an attentive and perhaps helpful sister. Three years older than Pierre, she told herself repeatedly that chronological justice destined him to turn to her for that assistance which he needed most, especially because of the Colonel's insanity and Mme. Dumont-Dufour's hatred, while at the same time she always forbade herself to imagine that Pierre might see something in her to put on a pedestal. But because she had spontaneously renounced the prospect of certain as yet unknown joys (about which she was unaware that ignorance made it easier to give them up) she had felt herself entitled to some compensation and had come to imagine that a subtle, sure link would always unite her heart and mind with Pierre's.

And so, during the dinner, the color that suddenly brought out the pale boy's good looks, the silence in which he shut himself, and his appetite as well, all gave Diane an impression of strength, a strength of which Pierre himself in his distraction had not yet become aware. She had a feeling that it was going to go against her, inexorably. She recalls that she smiled, when Mme. Blok, her hand over her heart in a pose as tragic as could ever be hoped for, depicting Pierre's arrival after Mme. Dumont-Dufour's exclamation, "He's simply a bit degenerate," said, "He entered the room like a thunderclap, with an evil, set look." Diane had echoed, "Poor little Pierre," and could scarcely imagine the boy with an evil, set look. But now she knows what her mother meant and knows she was right. There he is, in front of her, like a thunderclap, with an evil, set look. For the first time, she notices that Pierre has a heavy jaw and that, if he were to lose himself in God knows what craziness, the look in his eye would be as hard as the set of his mouth. Diane could easily be frightened. She thinks that Pierre will get up and leave as soon as they finish dinner. He has already become a stranger. Tomorrow Diane will be alone. She won't even have the courage to go back to the studio and keep on painting, she will spend her afternoons watching Mme. Blok knit and not understand. She will not attempt to find a substitute. When Pierre is lost she will not try to retrieve him in someone else. If she succeeds in forgetting him, it will be only to become a woman without attachments. She will live on, indifferent to everything and everyone, with nothing to live for except, to the end, the forlorn hope that he will return, a hope that will gradually turn into a dim memory.

But Diane for the moment wants to bank on her last chances. She resolves to shake her depression and try and outswim this invisible current of sadness that would sweep her so far away from her favorite person. Why think about a return that will gradually become a dim memory, when she may still have a chance to prevent Pierre from leaving at all, or at the very least, to catch him and bring him back? She will therefore stick to words and disregard all random thoughts save those which might conceivably serve as life buoys; and, since her silence and Pierre's are diverging and causing them to drift further and further apart, she attempts to rescue the situation with the first question that pops into her mind:

"Pierre, where are we going after dinner?"

"Shall we go to Bruggle's place?"

"Bruggle's?"

"Yes."

"But why?"

"I was supposed to have dinner with him. At the last minute he had to call it off, but he wants me to come over tonight."

"So you were supposed to have dinner with Bruggle?"

"Yes."

"Too bad."

"Why too bad? That's not fair, Diane. Look at what a nice person he is. It was Bruggle that said I should try and persuade you to come tonight."

Silence. Pierre turns red, tries to invent further reasons.

"You understand, it's absolutely necessary for me to go to Bruggle tonight. If I don't sleep at his place, where will I spend the night, because, you know, I walked out on my mother?"

"I thought so, Pierre."

"Did your mother tell you?"

Diane nods "yes" and looks at Pierre. Some rather affecting

DIFFICULT DEATH

vestiges of the child Pierre once was float across his face. Already
Diane wants to forget that during the entire dinner she must have
attributed her apprehensions to the boy's strange, silent mood.
She reproaches herself, as if for the most criminal complaisance,
for having slowly given in to certain fears, a coward. She had been
feeling sorry for herself, while Pierre, still hurting from the threats
Mme. Dumont-Dufour never failed to make, had been eating his
heart out in silence. Even if the poor kid does succeed in escaping
that hell whose tortures have been ceaselessly multiplied by the
Colonel's insanity and Mme. Dumont-Dufour's hate, what more
will he still have to go through? And Diane knows him to be so
ill-equipped, or rather, not equipped at all, for the struggle ahead:

"Poor Pierrot."

"Don't feel sorry for me, Diane."

"Listen, if you need anything at all…"

"I don't need anything."

"Do you at least have some money?"

"What a question! You're talking like my mother. You women
are all alike, you lose sight of the forest for the trees. Other than
money problems, nothing exists for you. Listen, Diane, Bruggle
isn't going to let me go without. He has already sold one of my
paintings for me. In this pocket is a wallet with a thousand francs."

"What's a thousand francs?"

"But I already told you, Bruggle isn't going to let me go without."

"Neither will I, Pierre."

Pierre says between clenched teeth: "I'm not a pimp."

Diane thinks she didn't hear the last word correctly:

"What was that?"

"Nothing."

A new silence. As she can think of nothing to say in reply, rather
than fault Pierre for his nastiness, or at least his nasty mood, she
rules that her own clumsiness is solely to blame.

Though not a word has been spoken that could undermine their
friendship, every minute makes the threat of silence heavier for
her. And she is willing to take upon herself the full responsibility
for the fainthearted farewell or the brutal and unnecessary quar-

rel that she is forced to foresee in a thousand details, the atmosphere of the dinner, and a certain unformulated but real premonition. Thus she can excuse Pierre's hostility, whose existence she can find no further reason to doubt. Let him persist in his sullen attempt to destroy everything between them, Diane will not stoop to those little tricks that are the best tactics in lovers' quarrels. Incapable of making up with the one she loves best, or even of countering his provocations with some fair response, Diane compares herself to the doctor who finds himself unable to treat a patient he loves too much using a remedy he would have thought nothing of prescribing for anyone else.

When Pierre exclaimed, "I have to sleep at Bruggle's," she exclaimed inwardly: "Beast! Not fair!" Had it been anyone but Pierre, she would have coolly judged: "Legitimate grounds for suspicion." And if he had not subsequently boasted that he had a thousand francs on him and declared (then repeated, with an insistence that was, to say the least, superfluous) that Bruggle would never let him do without, she would doubtless have succeeded in repressing the deduction that "I have to sleep at Bruggle's" meant in plain language, "I want to sleep with Bruggle."

Moreover, perhaps because, consciously or not, he had sensed Diane's unwillingness to draw conclusions, Pierre exaggerated until he felt that Diane would be forced to realize where she stood and admit it to her lasting sorrow. And she did indeed realize.

As for Diane, if she is hurt at Pierre's dotting the i's in this fashion, it is not that she is any more jealous today than she was yesterday – but the overly transparent periphrase that he used to banish her last doubts proclaims an aggressive hostility which (although she may explain or even absolve it) cannot fail to wound her deeply. And so, incapable of denying Pierre's malevolence, she tries nonetheless to take advantage of his last remaining scruples. And she who despises the little tricks of coquetry goes so far as to rack her brains to remember formulas for happiness, techniques guaranteed to dispel suspicions or prevent quarrels. Thus she recalls that children's manuals on deportment recommend taking a sip of water before getting angry, and, because she can feel the reproach-

DIFFICULT DEATH

ful words already on the tip of her tongue, she lights a cigarette and forbids herself to pronounce a single word or indulge in a single thought against Pierre until she has finished smoking the cigarette.

Once again, she will be the victim of her own good intentions. Because she is strong enough to observe a self-imposed silence and at the same time flex the tiny muscles that lift her nose, eyes, and mouth, and keep her face from sagging sadly, Pierre, who at bottom had perhaps orchestrated his companion's despair so effectively only the better to feel sorry for her in his turn, feels frustrated and angry, and it would not take much to make him claim that Diane is on the whole indifferent. Of the girl smoking in front of him, right next to him, with her mask of good resolutions so unlike the person he had expected she would be this evening, Pierre tells himself that the silence in which she armors herself in order to resist the spear-thrusts both of his silence and his words, is filled not with suffering but with spite. He is close to thinking that a deliberately malignant coquetry impels her to push things in the hope of more surely separating Bruggle and himself.

It is all in vain (he thinks) for women to feign curiosity, sympathy, or even admiration. We have seen several cases of that, all due to snobbery. They can never fail to feel pain and rage in the most intimate point of their pride, when they discover that the friendship of two men declares itself to the extent of becoming the love that hypocrites and the ignorant claim is possible only between members of opposite sexes. Diane, despite her charitable turn of mind, could only wish to despise the love I feel for Arthur. Because a love that she would spontaneously have judged impossible or ridiculous now impinges on her life, she can no longer content herself with the peaceable avenue of friendship, whose serene possibilities formerly sufficed. She has less affection for me now than hate for Bruggle. She will never forgive him for having caused me to discover that land of splendid torments, Love. Besides, no woman (Pierre repeats to himself) could think or act otherwise. Take that woman Arthur calls his "tamer," the

Rumano-Scandinavian countess. Far from taking offense at actions which she imagined were an expression of our sexual desires, she seemed to get a positive kick out of thinking about them. But then one day she suddenly took the opposite tack, started making fun of us, and at last flew into a rage as it became obvious that what was happening between us was no mere fantasy. If I slept with street hustlers, this Rumano-Scandinavian who professes freedom of thought would declare that I was a charming young man, she would rejoice and shout, "How colorful!" but let her see me madly in love with the strangest boy on earth, possessed but unwilling to be exorcised, and she is no longer capable of understanding.

As long as people think it's a vice, as long as they are looking for an amusing spectacle or at the very least an assortment of strange quirks which it is their pleasure to judge reprehensible but rare, like Oscar Wilde's orchids, then the reaction is one of respectful interest. But let someone come along whose sufferings in love are not betrayed by comical eccentricities or increased either by social persecution or the threat of prison or the dictates of fashion, but a man whose sufferings are wordless and quietly eat him up inside, people who were hoping for outlandish scenes, spicy anecdotes, scandalous gossip, will never forgive the commonplace simplicity of such a passion. The idea of my sleeping with Arthur is just as likely as not to amuse Diane, actually, but tonight she is in a rage with me because she has guessed that during this whole meal I have thought of no one but him. She could tolerate the merely physical side of it, and might even be somewhat aroused at the thought of how filthy and depraved it was, but even though she has told me a hundred times that there could never be any question of anything more than friendship between herself and me, she will never be able to stand my loving Arthur, or his loving me. She goes through the motions of renouncing any claim on my heart, but in fact she goes right on making up – or at least, trying to make up – new ways to get me away from Arthur. Under the pretext of helping me feel better, she cultivates what she thinks is my weakness, which so effectively highlights her strength. Often, even tonight, I have come dangerously close to letting myself go. It remains to be seen whether she will be equal to keeping this up much longer. I need to resist her. Without Arthur, I put myself in a young girl's hands, and acquiesced in a life with her that would have turned into a long sleep. But I would be living in the shadow of a shadow, because once she had got control over me, or rather whatever it is I represent to her, which for so many months was all she lived for, she would either want no more of me and jilt me, if not in fact at least in feeling, or, and this would actually amount to the same thing, she would become so docile as to be no more than a mirror, from which I would then get nothing at all beyond images of my own lonely mediocrity and of a faintheartedness that had managed to link its destiny with mine.

Diane isn't truly strong, she exists only by virtue of her relationship with me and by means of my obsessions which she claims to be helping me get rid of. The very source of the good she wants to do me lies in myself, not her, since, had she never met me in the first place, she would never have had the slightest notion of it. Bruggle, on the contrary, I love because he exists all by himself. His innermost self remains as invisible to me as the pit at the center of a fruit. As for myself, even though I obey him and comply with his slightest whims, he knows that he could break me on the wheel before I would betray my secrets to him. Diane, however, gave me hers spontaneously. Arthur and I play rough, we hurt each other. Nothing happens between us without a fight. In our love there is nothing decayed. We cut each other, our lips bleed, we break each other's jaws, but neither of us has ever got his teeth into the other's insides. He tortures me, beats me to a pulp, and the more we love each other, the more we are enemies; but neither really wishes the other to submit. It takes a woman, like Omphale, to make Hercules run away, and laugh to see him run.

From Bruggle, and all the days of being insulted and nights of being kicked in the teeth which I owe to him, came a first intimation of my own personal freedom. On the contrary, if I had fallen in love with Diane – and if I hadn't met Arthur, I'd have imagined I loved her and would have married her – it would have been as flat and not even as happy (consequently, even less excusable than) a life she might have led with any honest fellow, for example, the first chemical engineer who came along, someone like Edouard Cloupignon, whom her cousin Honoré Bricoulet wanted her to marry. In fact, why don't I mention this Cloupignon right now? Her vanity will be flattered. And since she herself acquiesced in the intrigues that were supposed to lead up to this marriage, she will not be able to go on reproaching me for Bruggle. Here goes:

"Tell me, Diane, are you still seeing your friend the chemical engineer? What are his chances?"

Diane lets her cigarette go out. She thinks Pierre is jealous; if he were not, he wouldn't give the chemical engineer a thought. Therefore, he cares for her and she was wrong to fear his indifference. As Pierre repeats his question, she smiles, all the happier in that she is less ready to feel in his peremptory tone and frown nothing but resentment at thinking of her being proud of a possible match, so that it is enough to pronounce the lucky man's name for her to be overjoyed.

Behind the mask she has at last found the man she loves the way she loves him. She no longer fears that he will let himself drift on a silence or vague words as deceptively soothing as they are hypnotic, on a groundswell leading, more likely than not, to Bruggle. Now that he has got his teeth into something concrete at last, he is no longer likely to get lost. If Cloupignon did not exist, it would be necessary to invent him. So she is thankful for Cloupignon, a memory imperceptible on the surface, a stumbling block that obliged Pierre when he bumped into it to come back to terms with his past, his true self.

Henceforth, all that had served Diane as an argument against Pierre becomes a proof of his affection. She was insane to take his every word so tragically, to read sinister intentions in every last thing he said. Where she was suffering from a supposed urge on his part to insult her to her face, he was only – however ungracefully – struggling to come out with it and tell her frankly what he felt. All those things that he had not managed to say tactfully now seemed to her to have been mere ranging shots whereby Pierre, torn between his passion for the transatlantic feline and his tenderness for the girl, wished to voice feelings of which it was only natural that he should want to be clear about them, in that they weighed so heavily with him.

Diane was never unaware, nor did she ever pretend to be unaware, that Pierre was in love with Bruggle, but tonight that love seems so improbable, so little in character with the person she wants to think Pierre is, that she decides it must be a disease and therefore curable. Then again, what difference does it make? Pierre's in love with her, after all – look at how insistent he is!

"Come on, what about Cloupignon? I want to know."

"You want to know."

"Yes, I want to know where I stand."

"You want to know where you stand."

She repeats his words with the air of a beggar-woman feeling the material of some beautiful new dress she is being given to wear. For him to think of demanding that she explain herself, at a time when he is himself at a difficult, possibly decisive moment of his life, is fairly reassuring, isn't it? A voice sweet with gratitude promises:

"I'll tell you everything, Pierre."

And is answered by a threat:

"You certainly are going to tell me everything, and if you don't tell the truth…"

"But I promise, I will tell you the whole thing. But you mustn't make fun of Cloupignon. That would be mean."

"Will you start?"

"Yes, Pierre. First, as you know, my mother's cousin Bricoulet comes every week on bended knee to ask her to marry him. I think actually she is dying to do just that, but knowing as she does that I loathe Bricoulet…"

"Why do you loathe him? I would like to point out to you, my dear Diane, that for all of your generous airs you are purely and simply destroying your poor mother's life. If you had a heart, you would put her hand in Honoré's and let the band strike up the Wedding March! I can see it all now – dear little Herminie in a Chantilly veil, a black satin sheath dress, a big crushed-velvet hat, bird of paradise plumes and – more Chantilly! – hat-veil, patent leather shoes, and two red carnations stuck in a silver fox. On Bricoulet's arm she climbs the staircase leading to the wedding hall of the fourteenth *arrondissement* municipal building. That same evening the newlyweds will leave for Italy, where they will spend their honeymoon. Yes, Diane, if you would only see where your duty lies…"

Diane cannot understand why Pierre has suddenly started clowning. She isn't sure whether he is making fun of her mother, Bricoulet, or herself. She is at a loss for an answer, when Pierre says, "Go on!"

"You tell me to go on and you'll interrupt me again."

"I'm not interrupting, I'm giving you my opinion. And you have such a charming family. Divine, in fact. Why would you have me abstain from savoring its qualities, when you are the first to rejoice over them? How happy Cloupignon would be, to stand up between Herminie and Honoré, and opposite his dear Dia-Diane. What a sensation the name Diane is going to make in your future home town!"

"Please, Pierre! First of all, I'm not engaged to Cloupignon!"

"What a relief. Do you remember the first time he came to dinner at your house and what a clever blow-by-blow you gave?"

"Pierre!"

"You were really in top form that night, more inspired than you are right now, in any case. I had only to hear you and I could see it all – your mother in her so-called Empress Eugénie hair bracelet, her pendant – a tiny basket of diamonds with ruby and sapphire flowers suspended from her neck by a platinum chain – which glittered so richly under the chandelier, all the lights of which the honest lady had turned on for the occasion. And do you remember Cloupignon's after-dinner story, told in that southern patois of his which you do so well:

DIFFICULT DEATH

" 'In the little rrestaurrant wherrre I eat, the cashier fell thrrrough a trrrapdoor into the cellar. What do you think she brrroke? Nothing, but she torrre something. Guess what she torrre.'

"Bricoulet: 'Her dress.'

" 'No.'

" 'Her corsage?' Mme. Blok ventures.

" 'No. You're both wrrrong. The cashier of the little rrrestaurrrant wherrre I eat, by falling thrrrough the trrapdoor into the cellar, torrre her *spleen*.' "

Pierre concludes: "God-damned Cloupignon – you're going to be the consort of a great mind!"

Diane cannot think of a retort to these sarcasms. She feels weak. She still thinks Pierre is jealous, and would willingly deliver Cloupignon up to him bound hand and foot if that would make him feel any better. In the meantime, in order to show him what she thinks of Cloupignon, she pulls a letter out of her handbag and passes it to Pierre, explaining:

"This is one of Cloupignon's letters. I made it clear to him that I hadn't the slightest desire to marry him, so he swore to conquer me. Every other day he writes. Tonight I got this diagram of his heart – kisses, arrows in red ink, little boxes..."

Diane said the last sentences very rapidly. She is frightened again. She doesn't dare look at Pierre as he says,

"Are you going to marry your friend Cloupignon, yes or no?"

"No."

"You're making a mistake. He's a clean cut, clearheaded, reasonable, well-behaved young man – just your cup of tea."

"Pierre, stop making fun of me."

"If you weren't basically attracted to the idea of marrying Cloupignon, you wouldn't be encouraging this correspondence. You wouldn't even open his letters – but – go ahead, admit it – you're really proud as Punch that a chemical engineer would deign to lay bare his heart to you – admit it!"

"Come on, Pierre, this isn't a laughing matter."

"Not a laughing matter? You're delightful. Who was it that repeated to me the story of the cashier with the torn spleen, and who is it that's showing me this minute a confidential calligraphic diagram of our dear friend Cloupignon's inner life? Diane, this comedy has gone on long enough. You haven't yet guessed that tonight I've had all I am going to take of our lies to each other."

"There are no lies. Neither of us should be accused of that. You have never lied to me, Pierre – I know all there is to know about you."

"You know all there is to know. Poor Diane. I, in any case, know more than enough. When you're with me, you make fun of Cloupignon, and when my back is turned, you sit with him, laughing at me. Tell me, what kind of funny stories do you tell him about me to make him laugh?"

"Pierre, please!"

"You tell him I'm in love with Bruggle. And this boy from Auvergne must be proud as Punch to think that he is marrying a woman who knows such unusual people. If you want to amuse him, point out that Pierre Dumont's initials – P.D. – predisposed him to the pederastic life he leads."

"Pierre, for God's sake, we're being overheard!"

"Overheard? You're really delightful. Because of three waiters and a couple of fat, half-drunk bourgeois who may or may not overhear what we're saying, you are refusing a necessary explanation."

"A necessary explanation? Ever since we sat down to dinner, you have done everything you could think of to start a fight. First you tortured me with your silence."

"I tortured you with my silence, what eloquence. My God, Diane, you talk just like a book."

"Pierre, you're making fun of me because you know you're in the wrong. But I want to forget you were nasty. You're unhappy."

"That's not true. I've never been so happy in my life."

Diane hangs her head. He takes her by the wrists and squeezes them until, when Diane raises her head, his eyes glaring into hers, he can shout it in her face:

"I've never been so happy in my life!"

Diane compresses her lips but cannot prevent two tears from slowly crossing her whole face.

DIFFICULT DEATH

Pierre does not notice her tears. Pierre sees nothing, hears nothing. He gets up, and Diane gets up, and they are both outside, side by side but not touching, like two parallel sleepwalkers who separately pursue their fateful course.

Pierre speaks: "I know that you are going to marry Cloupignon sooner or later, or someone exactly like him. The romance is over. I'm no superman, Diane, I'm just a poor sap and quite possibly diseased, too. But you, you're no amazon yourself. If you intend to persevere the way you're going, and continue your Sophie act as my nanny used to say, and choose for virginity and paint, all you'll succeed in doing in the long run will be to go rancid in chastity and an increasingly evil disposition. A pretty fate. I can picture the little drawing room on avenue d'Orléans where you will spend your solitary evenings. The time for salt-and-pepper hair (which you'll get cut too short) will come sooner than you think, and because already you won't dare study your mirror, you will reshuffle old memories so you can pretend you weren't attractive when you were young.

"But that doesn't mean that some fine day, on a train taking you to Florence or Granada or the like, you're going to be strongminded enough not to envy the young married couples around you; then you'll miss Cloupignon, by that time a Senator; then at long last you'll realize the true value of the effects of sunlight at St. Tropez, Pont Aven, Barbizon, flat-heeled shoes, tortoiseshell glasses, and the falsity of a love you will have relentlessly pretended to believe in. But how many more years are you going to wait before admitting to yourself that, basically, Nietzsche, Kant and the 'Critique of Pure Reason,' Oriental civilization, the problem of shadows and volumes, Philosophy with a big P, and Art with a big A, don't mean a fucking thing to you?

"Listen, Diane, as I told you, I've had enough of this lying. For a long time now I've intended to speak to you and each day I've put it off to the next. I have been frank with you (and even my frankness was, by the way, only relative) solely to conceal what was really in my mind. I haven't kept my actions or activities a secret from you, but I have always handled it in such a way as to

105

prevent you from getting a clear idea of anything, much less an inkling of what was going on in my head. The fact that you know the details of my private life and that I know yours has in no way kept our thoughts from remaining alien to each other. You know that I sleep with Bruggle and I, despite your excessively authentic-sounding slips, am well aware that you have never slept with anybody – but do you think that's enough? Our weakness was in refusing to face up to our own contradictions. And so, for a long time, out of cowardice, and to appease my conscience, I forced myself to think you were superhuman, but my bad faith was equally extreme, when this very evening I tried to find a way purely and simply to despise you. But what about yourself, Diane? Why adorn me with romantic graces? You wanted to deceive yourself about your own intentions and even now would as soon die as admit that if you got rid of Cloupignon it was only in hopes of marrying me one day. You make fun of the security, the peace and quiet your chemical engineer offers, but basically that's exactly what you'd like for you and me.

"It's high time you understood that you and I can never hope for anything like happiness with each other. Even if such happiness had been possible, you understand, Diane, you wouldn't have had from me any of that loving fidelity you dream about. I know that like all of those whose kingdom is not of this world, you drug yourself on the idea of happy fidelity. Forget it. Really, Diane, I can see now, I wouldn't have wanted you, I couldn't have stood living with you, even if you had been capable of giving me that peace which your voice, your hands, and all your tenderness towards me promised.

"Later, maybe, one day when our souls are no longer inside these bodies, fate will allow us to be joined in some transcendent bliss or other, but for the moment, here and now, admit that you have no choice but to despise those who get their wretched little pleasures after turning off the bedside lamp and kicking off their slippers; but the trouble with those wretched little pleasures is that never once, even in the most intense moments of your love for me, have you ever had the strength to imagine any others.

DIFFICULT DEATH

Even I, Diane, who would like to be drunk with agony, and spend my life repeating to myself that I love Bruggle for the dangers he represents – yet for thirty years of peace and quiet with him I would sell my soul. Not that in less than a week I wouldn't be able to stand the sight of him, if he ever stopped being the wild beast I am so frightened of and try by every means I can to tame.

"Diane, I'm asking you to forgive me, not for these words but for having taken so long to say them. I have only just come to understand that if you love me it's because you know I'm not for you. That's something both of us have suffered from; but, if all had gone smoothly between us, what mediocrities we would have been! Alas, we don't even have the right to pride ourselves on our sufferings, because if we have a certain notion of grandeur, it is in spite of ourselves – if it weren't for a fate we have both cursed time and again, neither of us would ever have had the courage to renounce the peaceful ways of mediocrity. Let us thank our honored parents – yours for his suicide and mine for his insanity. We both saw their wives thunderstruck, each in her own way, by a fate they thought inconceivable. They never got over it, any more than you and I ever will, for that matter. You and I, Diane, that's right, you and I, must admit that we had the great good fortune to have been capable of a bit of play-acting. I was never so happy in my life as I was the day it dawned on me that my father had lost his mind. My whole childhood had been such a bore. What a surprise it was that evening when he started insulting my mother: 'Virtue Louisa pumpkin you two-faced toad you gave me a dose of syph in the left ear.' My mother stared at him uncomprehendingly, but he got up without a word and grabbed his wife by the wrists, 'Murderess! Black-haired whore you'll pay for this!' I was so scared I shivered, but in the end I had the joy of knowing that to keep me amused in the future there would always be a little something in reserve in the way of food for thought.

"Later, when the theme of 'paternal insanity' was beginning to pall, I was saved by a series of nightmares in which the breasts of the floozies my school chums took me to see, all sorts of breasts, pathetic, proud, protuberant, pendulous, robust tanned ones, and

107

others pale as papier-mâché, all came loose from their owners' chests to torpedo me.

"When I woke up, it was only too simple to explain that Madame Dumont-Dufour's shrewish temperament had filled her son with a horror of prostitutes; the Colonel's insanity was in fact a mania for whores and it was to them that this hero, this captain, my father, owed the fact that he was in such a fine state on the road from one Ratapoilopolis to the next. And then, Diane, I met you – fresh, intelligent, kind-hearted, the exact opposite of those sluts who forced me to become aroused but never once overcame my disgust, and I believed I could actually fall in love with a woman – you. I would have liked to have a son by you. But one night, from a nightmare, I learned that it wasn't in order to love you through him that I had dreamt of him as being so attractive, too attractive. From that time on, I have been constantly frightened, and it's already been several months now that, if I had had enough of my health left to be an egotist, I wouldn't have gone on seeing you, I would have forced myself to stop thinking about you altogether.

"To be sure, I often said to myself that Bruggle was the sickness and you the remedy. That amounts to noting the fact that I didn't want or intend to recover.

"If you had decided on your own to marry Cloupignon, I would have been glad to be able to despise you and have nothing to say to you about this whole thing which is hurting you so much. Forgive me, Diane. Please forgive me. But maybe this evening even my crude actions and words have been less than frank. What if I complicated everything out of the fear of an oversimplification? There's a fact, Diane. Ever since I have known Bruggle, the rest of humanity (yourself included) has meant nothing to me. I would just as soon have killed the lot of you, destroyed you in a whole series of murders. Being sorry means nothing. This no longer has anything to do with happiness. I no longer have the strength or even the right, maybe, to feel qualms of conscience about anything. Am I hurting you? How could it have been any other way? Tell me which you prefer, knowing where you stand and having your wish for the raw truth come true, or putting things off again?

DIFFICULT DEATH

If you had known how I was suffering in the restaurant just now, in front of you, I didn't see you, but your presence made itself known because you were suffering and I could feel your pain around me like darkness, and it was only fair I should suffer from it since I was to blame. Bruggle is the sickness, you're the remedy. All right, but I don't want to recover, so what difference does it make? Diane, I can't go on. I'm scared. I don't even know how I got up the nerve to say this much. Diane, say something. I'm suffering, Diane, please swear you don't love me anymore so I won't be hateful to you. Diane, go ahead, say it, say you don't give a damn what happens to me. Diane, say something..."

Diane says nothing in reply. They continue like parallel sleepwalkers. Fog swirls round them and in it the girl's face looks like a swollen, sick fruit. Afraid of the silence, Pierre continues:

"If you only knew how much it meant for me to discover him. Wherever he goes, whatever he says or does, reproaches and guilt slide off him like water off a fish. He's the only person I know whose sole justification is in himself. The only one, Diane. I don't know if I deserved such a miracle. Remember last year, when I went on a trip with him? In the car, those summer afternoons, while he slept, so pure in his sleep he wasn't like a human being so much as a plant, I was ashamed of my own hands, hot and sad and dusty as they were. Mornings, on awakening, I didn't dare open my eyes or move closer to him and his warmth. He was the only one, the only earthly reality that could decide me to live without passing judgment on my life. When that life started, I was terrified that I would no longer recognize the person who was my sole reason for living. I was also terrified that he wouldn't recognize me, or would be unwilling to. At other times there was such a look of hellfire in his eyes I thought I'd burst into flames if he kept on looking at me that way. Do you know what I mean, to burst into flames, like dry straw, from someone looking at you? But Diane, as time went on, I started feeling guilty. Guilty about what? The pain I was causing you, I daresay. The pain I was going to have to cause you, sooner or later. Alone in my room, when I dreamed of Arthur's eyes, I'd see yours on top of them, reproaching me for not loving you enough. One night I got so scared, I got up and dressed. I rushed to his house. He started to bawl me out, but when he saw I was literally rigid with terror, he felt sorry for me. And then it was his fingers (his, you understand, Diane, his, not yours) that made me feel better. You see, he performs your miracles. You will never be able to perform his. And I can't do anything, anything at all for you; Diane, we've got to stop seeing each other."

"We've got to stop seeing each other," repeats an echo at his elbow.

Then the girl, still walking and staring, unseeing, straight ahead, hears a few jerky words, broken by sobs, begging her forgiveness. Moved to pity once again, she turns, sees Pierre standing still, a few steps behind, head in hands, weeping. Gently:

"Pierre, you mustn't cry."

He, between his teeth: "Diane, I'm ashamed of myself."

But she, like a refrain of consolation: "Pierre, you mustn't cry, you mustn't be ashamed of yourself. You have nothing to feel guilty about. I'm not blaming you for a thing. I'm your big sister, you know, nothing more than a big sister."

"Nothing but a big sister. Diane, I can't accept well-intentioned lies. Couldn't you swear to me…"

"Pierre, don't ask me to swear."

"You see, you still feel sorry for me. But I don't want any of your pity now, your good intentions are so transparent. Diane, your tenderness is no consolation for you and it does nothing for my misery, either."

"Let's not talk about your misery. You told me tonight you were the happiest of men. Bruggle's waiting for you. Go to Bruggle."

"I am going to Arthur's. But what about you, Diane?"

"I'm going home. Good-bye, Pierre."

"Good-bye, Diane."

Two hands touch without feeling; both seem colder than they would if they were dead. A girl walks stiffly away and is about to vanish in the fog. A boy shouts, calling her back. The girl stops, turns round, is about to go back, but the one who shouted – in-

DIFFICULT DEATH

voluntarily, it seems – exasperated with himself for the outburst, starts running, running away. Didn't he want her to turn around, the better to signify to her his wish for a final break between them. In an instant, the girl has lost even that surface courage that was sustaining her. She hurts without knowing where. Her feet drag.

Chapter Four

NIGHT, COLD, FREEDOM, DEATH

Within seconds Pierre is choking on the fog. As Bruggle has told him a hundred times, he doesn't know how to breathe. Even if the elements had been propitious to sprinters, after 100 meters he would have stopped just the same. Getting back his breath, he peers round as if afraid of being followed. He sees nothing and no one. He feels alone and free. Soon he is even laughing at his fears. Diane? Not even Diane would persist to the extent of galloping after a young man through the Paris streets at ten o'clock at night. Besides, by now at long last, she must realize where she stands.

Thanks to the Colonel's martial spirit and Mme. Dumont-Dufour's bellicose temper, from earliest childhood Pierre has been used to fights, even in the transactions of love or friendship; and so now that he has succeeded in jilting Diane (even though it was he who called her in the first place) he considers himself the winner, and congratulates himself on the perfect simplicity of his final, winning move. He prides himself on that move just as a stage designer might pride himself on a deft visual clue – a bit of ribbon arranged on a dark backdrop indicating a tree, a house, a mountain, a landscape. This dinner with Diane was truly, just as he was saying to himself a few minutes ago, a bridge from Mme. Dumont-Dufour to Bruggle, from lukewarm scruples to raw joy.

He has made a choice; he congratulates himself for having at last chosen, and chosen well. Mme. Dumont-Dufour, Diane, and Bruggle represented the three corners of a triangle and Pierre was wearing himself out running from one to the other. From now on, surrounded on all sides by Bruggle, he will forget how in the past he was running off at a tangent every day and growing paler all the time. A mud-splotched mirror glimpsed in the street to-night reveals a face that is still somewhat hollow-cheeked and green about the gills. But the new order of the day is Health. Let him at least look healthy starting this minute. Arthur must never again be able to make such cracks as "You look unwholesome!" which hurt his feelings so much in the past. Pausing under a street-lamp, he pinches his face and slaps himself until some pinkness colors his cheeks; then, when the initially pessimistic shop win-dow sends back a slightly less alarming image, in order to kill anxiety once and for all, three shots of cognac at the nearest bistro along the way. At last he hails a taxi and in no time arrives at Bruggle's house.

From the front door, snatches of a drinking tune remind him of nights in the slums, doors surmounted with letters outlined in bunches of electric lights, hotel signs that blink on and off (or rather, "wink," according to Monsieur Arthur), and the shaved necks, the red scarves, the cloth-topped boots with uppers made of some tastelessly light-colored material which never failed to arouse Arthur with his liquid eyes and nostrils wide open, hopped up on the smell of hot sweat, cherries in brandy, and young, easy-going flesh.

Pierre slowly climbs the five flights of stairs, his heart beating very fast. Already he imagines Bruggle in all his glory amid what he calls, with a smile that is not completely ironical, his "splen-dors." The studio is lit by Venetian lanterns, a whole wall solid with bottles and in counterpoint to the Steinway, a player piano which has supplanted the gramophone and the records. Thus Monsieur Arthur has created an atmosphere, the same as the one found in the dives where small-time boxers, pimps, and prosti-tutes of both sexes gather round the astonished American, in whose eyes they enjoy the freshness of novelty, curiosities to be used more intimately but otherwise of the same sort as African sculpture, psychoanalysis, and the Île Saint-Louis.

Pierre has never dared upbraid Bruggle for what he would call, if in a bad mood, Arthur's mania for camp, and yet tonight he sees nothing about it that is not somehow touching. He even smiles at the memory of a dinner, excruciating at the time, with Bruggle and a juvenile delinquent who had been billed as a great artist who could play up a storm on the accordion.

This virtuoso from La Villette was at the time doing a hitch in the Navy, thanks to which he was able to take the best advantage of his reasonably smooth, fresh skin to drive anyone insane who was susceptible to heart failure at the sight of a sailor's cap with a red pom-pom. Moreover, his natural vigor very effectively protected him from the fatigues or qualms that might have spoiled the profits that his youth, the art of making goo-goo eyes, and the encouraging facility with which he promptly shared the desires that his person had begun to arouse allowed him to add to his five francs daily. The uniform, because anonymous, makes it easier for youths to dispense their charms freely, even conferring on them a certain hypocritical dignity; and so, when this rogue was on leave, Monsieur Arthur, who loved to impress, decided to take him to dinner in a fancy restaurant where, until that day, bell-bottoms, jersey scarves with loud flower patterns, pink silk shirts, and two-tone shoes had barred him access. Whereupon, disoriented by the brightness of the chandeliers, and the imposing manner of the maître d', the little sailor who had no idea how to rest his good sturdy accordion-player's mitts on the white tablecloth or how to handle a certain disconcerting fork in order not to look idiotic or out of place between Bruggle and Pierre who were manfully helping themselves to more fish from the serving platter, or what to do when a woman entered, or a new dish was brought on, observed with that disdain whereby innocent souls hope to create an impression of ease and freedom, "I knows of better but it costs more." And every time he said it, Monsieur Arthur would echo him with a laugh that got louder as his mood

DIFFICULT DEATH

became increasingly jovial: "The better it is, the more it costs!"

After dinner, a walk to the Fairgrounds where Pierre didn't want to visit the waxwork museum. The other two took that opportunity to lose him. As always, he refused to believe in any malice aforethought on his elusive friend's part, and went to Bruggle's house, convinced he was expected there. The door to the apartment was ajar and in this negligence Pierre read a friendly message, until the instant when, on the threshold of Bruggle's bedroom, he saw Monsieur Arthur who was dancing, the sailor's cap on his head, while the latter, a glass in hand, perfectly reminiscent of a bar on the Quai Cronstadt, at the water's edge, crooned to himself:
When I'm in your arms...

And Monsieur Arthur, as though he had made up his mind to say or sing nothing that the accordion-player would not have said or sung to continue his solitary Charleston, accompanied with a tune that a Parisian gigolo had taught him one deliciously ambiguous evening in Toulon.

When Bruggle finished, he noticed Pierre's presence at long last.

"Hey, Pierre, what's up?"

"Nothing."

"Do you want something?"

"No."

"Sit down."

"No."

"Don't pull a long face here. If you don't like it, get out. This is my home. I have a right to my freedom. I like people to respect that right."

"You talk about your freedom. You ought to say your vanity."

"Hey, that's enough!"

Thereupon Pierre strangled on his words, lost all coherence, blacked out, bit, kicked, punched, spat, and screamed insults, until the accordion player got out of there bag and baggage.

From that day on, Pierre could have sent every one of Bruggle's dear little boxers packing, although elsewhere he was more highly esteemed for having (with conscious and calculated coquetry, moreover) quoted the opinion of that heavy-weight, his kindly physical education instructor: "Just 'cause you're a peculiar little bird ain't no reason to think you don't make the grade."

But tonight, having at last arrived at Bruggle's landing, only a few seconds, a few feet from the beloved, he is unwilling to let a vulgar pianola condemn him to fresh anxiety attacks. He no longer remembers a bit of his chronic hatred of his mother; he has forgotten how bored he could get with Diane. If he has quarreled with his mother and run away from Diane, he would like to believe he did all this for someone who really deserved to have the others sacrificed for him. His love is like a stained-glass window whose luminous transparency has changed the color of his whole life, from its most grandiose themes down to the pettiest details. That same love will however turn into a sad, dingy flake of mica unless he can persuade himself that he is logically, nay mathematically, deserving of it. Thus he expects that the moment he walks in the door Bruggle will provide some immediate concrete proof that he was not wrong to prefer him to the others.

Pierre reaches for the door. His fingers are quivering so hard they drum against the doorknob, not with fright but with happiness.

Inside, a dozen couples are dancing. The host is mixing cocktails. The Rumano-Scandinavian countess is shimmying ecstatically in the arms of a young punk. An American woman is explaining at the top of her lungs that her apartment consists of only two rooms but the walls of one of them are completely covered with all her earrings. She calls Pierre to witness, and Pierre, who has not yet even said hello to Bruggle, is obliged to describe the endless rows of Venetian pearls, balls, rings, lozenges, tiny gold and silver animals, crystal drops, which the pretty collector from across the Atlantic sticks first in plaster and then in her earlobes.

The player piano stops at the end of a roll, and Pierre takes advantage of the lull to join Bruggle, but immediately the Rumano-Scandinavian is on top of them, overflowing with praises for her dance partner: "His name is Totor – nineteen – and what a beauty! A poet, too. Anyhow, poet and punk are the same thing. All true artists are poets. All true poets are punks. Arthur Bruggle, my dear, you are a great composer, but if you weren't such a darling *crapule* at heart..."

"What is *crapule?*" Bruggle demands to know.

The Rumano-Scandinavian smiles: "Oh, darling, a *crapule,* a great, big, sweet *crapule* like you is the same as a hooker with a rose for a heart. A rose of pink, gold, and bright green paper – isn't that so, Pierre? You know him, you must admit that our Arthur's a hooker with a rose heart."

Pierre blushes and nods affirmatively.

Monsieur Arthur is about to have what he calls a stupor. Monsieur Arthur makes a face. He doesn't quite know whether he ought to fly into a rage or laugh. "My tamer is beastly rude," he often says. And the fact is, this hyperactive fifty-year-old steeps herself in cucumber lotions in vain – their unction will never get past her skin. To make and break reputations, to affect the behavior and language of a camp follower, to suck on her Abdullah cigarette like a pukka old soldier on his clay pipe – these were on the whole the best of her predilections. Thus, whereas Pierre claims that if she confined herself to her camping and did not have that "diamond in the rough" side, she would be unbearable, Monsieur Arthur to the contrary exclaims, "Her deliberate bad manners are idiotic and will ruin my reputation or at the very least may make me miss out on my big chance." Then he goes on to explain he is perfectly willing to be a gilded youth but is primarily interested in being a composer. The Rumano-Scandinavian bursts out laughing amid a cloud of smoke from her Turkish cigarette and teases Bruggle until, glimpsing a hint of savagery in his face, she calms him with a "Dear boy, you're the Beau Brummell of the dance halls," or some bromide to the same effect.

Monsieur Arthur still fears he is being laughed at:

"You're making fun of me."

"No, dear."

Then, his fears put to rest, he savors the compliment: the Beau Brummell of the dance halls. "Do you really think those twits pay attention to me and think I'm elegant?"

"They adore you, dear."

RENE CREVEL

Monsieur Arthur is in seventh heaven. The Brummell of the music halls. Monsieur Arthur is a winner. He doesn't mind having people notice he dislikes being called a "hooker with a rose heart" even if that were only to force him to note that if he is a winner, it isn't as though he weren't trying. For his tamer to be rude was bad enough. He could take that. However, for Pierre to back her up is enough to raise his hackles in earnest. So he scowls and mutters, "Bullshit!" between his teeth. To forget this reproof, Pierre gulps down his drink in one swallow, and the Rumano-Scandinavian continues:

"Isn't my dancing partner a dream? Bruggle and I found him in a club at porte des Lilas. Not some tourist trap – the real thing. It's called 'The Randy Rabbit.' Isn't that a great name? All the street people, the gay ones, get together there and grind till they lose their mind. Gay street people – how about that – outrageous, huh? Totor is a street person and just look how elegant he is. I don't know of a dancer fit to tie his shoestrings in the entire Court of Denmark. Totor has a friend, a mate as he calls him. If you could only see them dance, Totor and his mate (I adore that word). Armand is his name, nicknamed Hari-Kari because he was stabbed. He's that short, stocky one over there by the Steinway, with Lucas. Say, Arthur, darling. Totor and Hari-Kari could do a little number for us right now. Their waltz is fabulous. I'm going to get the director of the Danish Ballet to hire them. It's better than Nijinsky. Less literary, above all.

"And to think that devil Lucas, who's always disagreeing with everyone, keeps saying anything that comes into his head to put us off our gay friends from the Randy Rabbit. But look – I don't believe it! – he's talking to Totor's mate."

She yelled across the room to the man called Lucas, whom until that moment she had detested, because he had never yet had the grace to change fads with every changing season, nor to share, according to the taste of the day, his contemporaries' enthusiasm for opium dens, Oxford trousers with outsized cuffs, and dance clubs of so-called ill fame:

"Hey, Lucas, don't monopolize Hari-Kari! You've no right to

him anyway, since you claim to like women. Arthur, dear, start up the player piano and let's go."

Bruggle's guests have gathered round. Very well, Bruggle snaps. Armand and Totor have already started dancing.

Monsieur Arthur feels it would be superfluous to make an introduction. With a loud "Shhhh..." he silences every sound save for that of the mechanical piano. Drunk with success, Totor and Hari-Kari turn round and round, pressed tightly in each other's arms. An invisible current propels them along; they follow its slightest whims; then, suddenly, coming back to the basic beat, a couple united against the world (all the way from the weather to human society, and a music whose thread can often be a snare), they draw themselves up, stamping mad temptations underfoot and, in a march, each step of which could be counted by menaces, seem to be passing their invisible but reliable allies in review. The Rumano-Scandinavian breathes it all in, her nostrils flaring, her bosom heaving, like an ancient Roman trainer of wild beasts, savoring the smell of his entire menagerie. Bruggle, from time to time, closes his eyes, to have the surprise on opening them once more, of seeing the dancers poised on the perilous peak of a musical phrase. Pierre is as pale as a sheet. Lucas, standing at Pierre's elbow, whispers, "They make me laugh with this juvenile delinquent mystique of theirs! I bet you heard our Rumano-Scandinavian claim Armand was nicknamed Hari-Kari because he was stabbed. Forget it! Armand himself just told me he got it from an appendix operation. I can't for the life of me understand this taste they have for slumming and fifth-rate queer bars."

"I know, I know," Pierre mutters in reply. He has just glimpsed Arthur and Totor exchanging glances.

He knows...

Arthur the foreigner and Totor the Parisian apache. Like Valenciennes lace, Cambrai taffy, Commercy madeleines. The Randy Rabbit, where queer street people congregate. He laughs to himself. Could the Rumano-Scandinavian, who could fool the devil himself if she felt like it, be subject to lapses now and again? Totor and (as she put it) his "mate" Hari-Kari dance on, like wind-up toys, lewd robots of flesh and blood that Bruggle's guests would like to think dangerous. Arthur gazes at Totor.

Pierre is losing all patience at seeing Arthur contemplate Totor with the same admiration he bestows on Quattrocento paintings, the music of Bach, and parlor metaphysics. Is the world nothing but a game for Arthur? Whatever it is, he has never watched Pierre move as attentively as he is now watching this hustler. But at the very same time as jealousy chokes him up, Pierre forces himself to smile. Granted, he reasons, that he would sacrifice the whole world for one person and forgive that person the most enormous crimes, it would be insane to begrudge him a flirtatious look, much less get upset and suffer over it. Arthur is making eyes at Totor, so let him take this Totor and do with him as he pleases. Any action or thought expended on this twit amounts to nothing more, actually, than the fact of a child putting his teddy bear on his pillow next to him. Arthur, Totor, the names of the composer from across the Atlantic and of the young hustler are charms against anger. They remind Pierre of the match-stick people that filled the pages of the Thursday funny papers back in the red-balloon period of his life. In the player piano, the waltzing couple, and the guests whom the Rumano-Scandinavian has herded into a circle round the dancers, in the whole thing considered by Monsieur Arthur with so much seriousness, nay, passion, is there anything happening, truly, that would be out of place in any kindergarten?

Pierre finds the childishness of it all the more touching in that Bruggle often says, by way of an almost fatherly rebuke: "You're so infantile."

And indeed, Pierre, who is clumsy with objects and facts, and too candid to be willing to use people, is at times quite close to thinking that his private fears and even the general anxiety that he would happily qualify as metaphysical anxiety don't amount to any more in human terms than the fear of getting lost in the Bois de Boulogne or the Luxembourg Gardens that haunted him when he was three years old.

For Monsieur Arthur, who sees, hears, and breathes the way

DIFFICULT DEATH

people are supposed to see, hear, and breathe (and due to that fact has never doubted the testimony of those all-too-faithful servants, his senses), sights, sounds, and the air he breathes declare their separate respective truths, which he would be incapable of doubting, and which, in all honesty and with an infallible intuition, he attempts to adapt to his own greater comfort. And thanks to what he calls his "idea of the realities," he never misses an opportunity to do just that. This art of accommodating people and things to one's own advantage is a sign of an innocence Pierre knows he will never attain. Bruggle will always be at his ease in a world in which he discovers comical resemblances, and Pierre is touched and amused to have been compared to one or another boy in the same way as the player piano in Bruggle's studio might have been compared to the one in a certain dance club.

If Arthur has chosen a table of a given model for his room, it is because in his opinion this particular table is in itself superior to all others. Not for one minute will he be tempted to suspect that the object of his preference derives its value solely from his liking for it. Likewise, even though he is as fickle as can be, he justifies his desires, rages, and infatuations by the feeling that he is acting in obedience to a hierarchy of values which he pictures as being brightly colored, like a comic strip.

Hence a system of parallels and levels.

He never stops holding up examples to Pierre. And his very need to compare Pierre to someone else proves that, despite a whole card-deck full of cruel tricks, he still feels tenderness, maybe even admiration for Pierre.

On his side, Pierre, despite his continuing submissiveness, acknowledges responsibilities from which he judges Bruggle exempt. He accepts responsibility for the man and the woman of whom he is an extension, while Bruggle on the contrary is not tied to his background. The reason for this is that the children of the old countries, even if they sometimes happen to attain freedom and innocence, are never born either free or innocent.

And so, whereas Pierre is helpless against certain shocks of anxiety, Bruggle on the contrary, however unmanageable he may continue to be, will always be capable of parrying the thrusts of misfortune with arguments based on the simplest common sense. Once he sees that it lies in his own best interests to let himself be convinced, he will savor the security of this or that scientific theory as readily as when he takes objects and situations by their smooth handle, the better to live with them. No phantoms of superstition will ever terrify Bruggle. His nights will perhaps be haunted, but when he gets the horrors, there will be no echo to plunge him into the past or future. A boy savage, all the more of a savage in that he contents himself with a theory like a Negress with a necklace of glass beads, when Pierre tells him about fears that transcend words, things, or present persons, he will reply that that's no reason to worry oneself sick, a man who has got any self-control at all won't get caught up in any such vague romantic nonsense. Bruggle's most powerful argument is that man is descended from the ape, and when he talks about Darwinism and the court case recently brought by reactionaries in the United States against a young high school teacher, a convinced partisan of Evolution, his manner is so cocksure that all of Pierre's sympathies go to those who believe that woman was made from Adam's rib and take literally all the rest of the Biblical metaphors. Moreover, the moment he speaks of the mysteries of the mind, this man from across the Atlantic (in whom, however, beneath his armor of facile logic and æstheticism, one is forced to recognize the most endearing contradictions) thinks he has got an answer in the preemptory arguments with which he describes the life of amœbas or the procession of the stars, and he is unwilling to pay any attention when Pierre declares that in reality Bruggle's fear of the unknown is the one and only reason he has all these scientific theories served up hot off the press, in order to relegate to the past a mystery which the Ancients for instance thought they were explaining when they said that the earth rested on an elephant, the elephant on a camel, the camel on a tortoise, and so forth.

"Bullshit!" exclaims Monsieur Arthur, who might just fly off the handle if this continues. Pierre has been listening to him with all the fondness of a mother when her little one recites fairy tales or saints' lives. Pierre is no longer annoyed with him for calling him "so infantile." He smiles at Monsieur Arthur and the latter sees in this sudden warmth a mark of submission, an admission that he is wrong, or an acknowledgment of inferiority. Thus, whereas Bruggle is more than ever convinced that Pierre is "so infantile," Pierre on his side thinks he must be indulgent with Bruggle, who is no doubt a great composer but has retained that same open-heartedness and endearing puerility that Negroes have. Unfortunately, Pierre may repeat to himself until he is blue in the face that Bruggle will in every respect be as innocent as a newborn babe as long as he lives, but all in vain – Pierre cannot help suffering from the actions and words by which this innocence expresses itself, an innocence whose face could at times be easily mistaken for that of hardheartedness or even sadism.

Further, because he likes Bruggle's youthfulness more than anything else about him, Pierre is not unaware that this quality is less a matter of animal grace, loud laughter, or the need to shake his body than of that childlike self-centeredness that prevents him from realizing he has done a wrong thing, an unkindness. Thus Monsieur Arthur, at the very moment when he is exhibiting the most unnecessary kind of rudeness, will be convinced that he is the soul of sweetness and light, or alternatively may feel that he is strengthening his position by reacting to something with exaggerated indifference or gratuitous contempt, and – without even noticing the paradox – will quite seriously rejoice at being nicknamed the Beau Brummel of the dance clubs, for to him it is no trifling matter to reign over the little world of boxers and pederastic riffraff in the nightclubs around porte des Lilas. Likewise, each time Pierre calls him "Monsieur Arthur," he gets a "new awareness of his dignity," and Pierre allows himself to be touched by this "new awareness," only to suffer all the more, one might say, from the wandering eye and corresponding words and actions whereby that awareness manifests itself. Moreover, Monsieur Arthur, who is fond of saying in any connection, "I know how to teach people their manners," thinks nothing of bawling Pierre out in public, particularly when reproaching him for a lack of courtesy to the habitués of the dives where they go slumming, where he drags Pierre only because he is not sufficiently sure of himself and his mastery of French to venture there alone. Especially when in his own apartment, he insists that the most gracious condescension should be shown his guests from porte des Lilas, whose shaved necks, red scarves, skill as dancers, and slang he holds in an esteem that is all the greater in that the Rumano-Scandinavian, for whom basically he has a deep respect, declares that her perverted young boxers are artists, dancers of genius, and poets, too, even greater than Nijinsky whom she nevertheless considers the most godlike man of all peoples or times.

Thus Bruggle and his "tamer," because they have invited a handful of snobs to watch a couple of juvenile delinquents bump and grind to the sound of a pianola, imagine themselves to be prophets, and once the dance is over, while Monsieur Arthur explodes with admiration, the Rumano-Scandinavian punctuates her bravos with shouts of "Fantastic, dear!" Totor and Hari-Kari make their bows. They are flushed and sweating. Bruggle pulls a magnificent handkerchief (a gift from Pierre) out of his pocket to wipe Totor's brow. A moment later, when Totor starts to hand it back, Bruggle says, "Keep it."

Pierre turns pale. Arthur will soon perceive that he is drinking in a corner by himself, glassy-eyed. He calls, "Hi, Pierre! Getting bored?"

"No, Arthur."

"Then why are you pulling such a face? You look as though you were about to go into a stupor. Come on, let's dance a little bit."

"Yes, Arthur."

"It's really not right for you to get drunk like this, all by yourself in a corner. Also, you really might have congratulated Totor and Armand on their dance. Wasn't it magnificent?"

"Yes, Arthur."

"Then why didn't you tell them that? I don't like your attitude. The kids from porte des Lilas have more manners than rich kids. Go pay them your compliments and ask Totor if he would like you to paint his portrait."

DIFFICULT DEATH

"I don't have the time right now to do a portrait of your friend Totor."

"My friend Totor? Come on, Pierre, let's not have any jealous fits. Don't do your number tonight."

"Please, Arthur."

"If you're in a bad mood, if you're tired, you can leave, but don't spoil my party."

"I'm not spoiling your party."

"If you say so. But I know you're going to ruin it. You would do better to leave now."

"You want me to leave so you can stay with Totor."

"That's none of your business. I have a right to my freedom."

"Your freedom is nothing but vanity."

"Go to hell."

"You're the one who started it. I didn't say a thing."

"You didn't say a thing but there was something insolent about your silence. I want people to be polite to my friends."

"I don't even know where your friends Totor and Armand come from."

"I first met them in a club at porte des Lilas, the 'Randy Rabbit,' " says Bruggle in the same tone in which he might have said, "I first saw them at a reception given by Duchess X or Princess Y."

Pierre makes no reply. Arthur persists.

"OK, go congratulate them."

"No."

"You're not polite. You have no tact."

"I daresay you have a lot of tact, yourself, giving away the handkerchief I gave you to the first hustler that walks in off the street."

Arthur suddenly shows his evil look, the one he wears on days when he feels he is in the wrong but is unwilling to give in and does not know what to do so that his charm will go to work and overcome. It is at such times that he speaks of his rights, states that he is an artist, boasts of being a savage and a gentleman simultaneously, and raises his voice to crush all opposition with a "Bullshit!" or "Shut up!"

The Rumano-Scandinavian, scenting trouble, mixes in:

125

RENE CREVEL

"Lovers' quarrels..."

Bruggle explains, after a fashion: "Pierre isn't being a nice person. He's trying to ruin my party. He doesn't know how to act in polite company. He hasn't even congratulated the dancers, and he isn't willing to do a portrait of Totor."

The "tamer" tries coaxing Pierre:

"Oh, *do* a portrait of Totor, darling! I'll buy it."

"I'm not doing Totor's portrait."

"Why not?"

"Because I can't stand him."

"He can't stand Totor, a perfectly nice kid."

"Please let me be."

"Pierre, you don't know what you're missing out on. I sold a picture for you. You don't have any money and yet you refuse to do Totor's portrait and talk back."

The Rumano-Scandinavian tries cooing some more:

"Listen darling, both of them are scrumptious..." She continues in a whisper, with cloying sweetness: "Let me introduce you to little Hari-Kari. It will work out perfectly. Arthur will spend the night with Totor. And you can have Hari-Kari."

Pierre's lips are compressed.

"All right?"

He persists in his refusal to answer.

He is left by himself. Arthur starts the pianola once more and starts dancing with Totor. A dance: Arthur and Totor. The names Arthur and Totor are no longer charms against anger. Arthur and Totor, entwined in each other's arms, spinning round and round, reeling and falling against random chairs, glued to each other in an ecstasy in front of Pierre who is still desperately seeking some means of quelling his jealousy. Arthur and Totor are no longer the little matchstick people from the Thursday funny papers of the red-balloon era of one's life. Totor leads. Arthur has doffed his smoking jacket and vest, and glides across the floor, his chest pressed to the young hustler's. Their two faces are cheek to cheek, their legs touch. They brush past Pierre, and he overhears something like "nice pimp, sweet pea..." Pierre feels a pounding against his ribs on the left side. He must have had too much cognac. Bad for the heart. Arthur clasps his fingers over a shaved neck. The young hustler's hands disappear beneath a silk shirt to rejoice in a skin all too familiar to Pierre. In vain he pours himself a slug of gin and knocks it back in one swallow, his eyes closed: when the eyelids go back up, the scene is unchanged. The dancers' desire for each other has only become more visible. Egged on by the Rumano-Scandinavian, Monsieur Arthur has let his shirt slip down round his waist. Against Arthur's naked torso the dancer presses his teeth and gluts himself, his nose flattened against Arthur's skin, as pleasant a blindfold as he could ever hope for, one that gives him the audacity to hide nothing of his desire and to continue with dance-steps that leave no room for doubt.

When the pianola stops, Pierre wonders how they will ever separate the dancers. A circle forms round the immobile but still united couple. Totor's teeth are unwilling to relinquish their prey (whose exact scent is so well known to Pierre). Monsieur Arthur, his eyes totally distended, moans. The little hustler's aggressiveness flatters him, and while his legs squeeze the other's hard enough to break them, his chest offers itself, a happy victim, to the other's nails. The guests miss nothing of the scene. The Rumano-Scandinavian is beside herself with enthusiasm, overjoyed. She appoints Hari-Kari arbiter of taste, exclaiming, "Isn't it lovely, dear! You have a right to be proud of Totor—he is really marvelous!" The American woman with the earrings laughs at the top of her lungs and throws big friendly kisses to the two boys, encouraging them as if it were a game: "Keep it up, kids!" Meanwhile, as Lucas shrugs and swallows his exasperation, Pierre, alone in his corner with his drink, is pleased to see that Lucas shares neither the joy nor the curiosity of the others, but maintains a mournful aloofness from everything and everyone. This day is decidedly a day of liquidations: Mme. Dumont-Dufour and Diane, representing hate and friendship respectively, and now Bruggle and love. A few more drops of alcohol and he will have achieved the absolute in indifference. Therefore, Freedom. And doubtless boredom, too. Who cares if it is boring? Three cheers for Freedom. For Bruggle,

RENE CREVEL

freedom means being desired by a little street-hustler. All jealousy aside, Pierre can scarcely imagine that this dubious teenager unearthed in a fifth-rate queer bar is much of a bargain. "I knows of better but it costs more," as the accordion-playing sailor said, the one with whom Arthur connived to get rid of Pierre at the fair. That night Pierre succeeded in getting rid of the sailor. Tonight he will behave. He abandons Monsieur Arthur to the hustler from the "Randy Rabbit." Bruggle has chosen his new love. Too bad for him! "I knows of better but it costs more." He'd better not complain. He's got his "freedom." And for him "freedom" means a dance with Totor. His freedom's name is Totor. Pierre's will have only one name. The best there is. I knows of none better and there's none costs more. He doesn't dare name it, though, even now that his life is ebbing rapidly. One more drink, one more hit of oblivion. Let the other have himself bitten on the chest, neck, back, legs, crotch, as much as he likes. Pierre doesn't give a fuck. Pierre is free. His freedom is Death. Death's the best there is, none better. In just a bit, very soon, he will leave by himself. The river isn't far from Arthur's house. There, from a bridge...

"Come, dear, we mustn't sulk..." It's the Rumano-Scandinavian who has come over to take him to task. She just can't let him be. Nevertheless, she is in for a big disappointment – she will never be able to put him into a rage again. Already he is trying to think of something to say that will startle her:

"No, no, I'm not in a bad mood, really. I'm just leveling out. When I got here, I was depressed. I've performed a miracle because now I'm feeling great – never felt better!"

He hears his own voice. He had intended it to sound menacing. Instead, his voice rings false, brittle as glass. The Rumano-Scandinavian looks him straight in the eye. She, for one, is not about to be intimidated. In a decisive tone she states: "Arthur is outrageous. My dear, he's quite right, you know, to call himself 'the boy savage.' What a magnificent beast, though! I've been told he called me his 'tamer' but neither you nor I will ever tame this tiger. Look at him right now – dancing with Totor again! Isn't it splendid, dear?"

DIFFICULT DEATH

So Pierre was right to wonder how they would ever separate the dancers – they should probably just give up on it. Arthur and Totor are condemned to spend the rest of their lives stuck together. Why not? There's one person at any rate who couldn't care less, and that's Pierre Dumont. The couple, brushing past, jostle him. Pierre smiles. No, not quite. He doesn't smile, he hangs a smile between his cheekbones. Diane used to pin on fake smiles in just this way. Diane. It was Pierre's fault, nobody else's, that the girl tried to mimic a joy he was making impossible for her. His fault. He sacrificed Diane. For whom? For a little American who arrived in France as a dishwasher whose happiness and freedom consist of dancing stripped to the waist with a male hustler. Pierre really has very little to be proud of. What he's getting now serves him right. He may have put on a smile but the mask is all too transparent. The couple jostle him again. Now they seem to be trying to get a rise out of him. To force himself to remain indifferent, Pierre digs his nails into his palms. A poor remedy. The couple make a mistake and jostle him a third time, when the nails that were torturing their own palms drop these in order to enter a neck, Arthur's neck, while a pair of feet begin their work of rage and vengeance despite surprised murmurs of pain. Totor and Arthur, separated at last, shake Pierre who screams insults and is unwilling to let go of his hold on Arthur's neck. Bruggle's guests intervene. Pierre's fingers are forced to abandon a neck in which they are imprinted in purple. Pierre himself is absolutely white; his lips quiver. The Rumano-Scandinavian, secretly rejoicing at this scene but unwilling to let it go any further, tries to calm him down:

"Come, dear, no foolishness..."

"No foolishness! Why don't you just shut up, you old bag!"

"Watch your manners, please. You forget who you're talking to."

"I'll say what I like. You've always done your best to separate Arthur and me. You brought these filthy hoods up here."

"Insult Arthur's friends as much as you please, dearie. I'm not mixing in your private affairs. Arthur is a big boy now. He can have his fun where he pleases. Is it my fault you made him lose patience with your little-girl tantrums? You're worse than a child, you're ten years old."

"I know someone who would be happy if she could say the same."

"Arthur! Do you hear the filthy way he's attacking me?"

So Arthur, who has put his shirt back on and recovered an awareness of his dignity, makes his eyes bulge impressively and says in a big voice:

"You may leave now, Pierre, now that you have ruined my party. Oh, you really shouldn't have done that."

"I ruined his party! Do you hear, he finds nothing else to say to me! I ruined his party. All that matters, then, is a few snobs and comic-opera fairies. You'll never understand. You're going to hate me for the rest of your life because I spoiled your big chance. But, Arthur, don't you know there's other things than the Danish Ballet and a few chic successes? Arthur, Arthur…"

He no longer has the strength to continue. At the last words he breaks down like a little kid. He is ashamed to be crying in front of the Rumano-Scandinavian and Arthur, both of whom are laughing. The two teenagers make fun of him, mimic his tears and "Arthur, Arthur…" The Rumano-Scandinavian shifts gears from a snicker to a hearty laugh, her mouth wide open, her head thrown back. Lucas silences the hustlers, then, gently, to Pierre: "We'll walk you home, but we'd better get some air first. Tomorrow nobody will remember a thing."

Pierre has lost all willpower. He lets himself be dressed like a baby. Lucas nods to tell him they will leave together.

He is led outdoors. The shock of the cold air quiets him down. He moans, and Lucas, that wholesome type, tries to soothe him…

Pierre explains in a faraway voice:

"If you had left me there, I would have gone on insulting them all night. I would have wanted to break the whole thing off between him and me, but I would never have had the courage simply to leave. I was his slave. I gave myself false reasons to try and believe I wasn't wrong to love him so much. I insulted his countess so he wouldn't forgive me or want to see me again. Yes, it's all over now. I'm happy, free…"

In a murmur, for himself alone, he repeats the phrases from a few minutes ago, when Bruggle was dancing with the hustler. "Arthur's freedom is named Totor. I knows of better but it costs more. My freedom's the best there is, my freedom is…"

Already he no longer dares pronounce that word. One arm tightly clasping Lucas' arm, his eyes filled with tears, he feels himself turning back into a child. Then he hears Lucas' voice, patiently explaining: "Arthur cares for you. He's a young, untamed animal. His cruelty just goes to show how innocent he is." Pierre nods yes. Hasn't he already put forward the same argument a thousand times, in order not to hate Monsieur Arthur? Exactly: Arthur is a wild animal, and his cruelty just shows how innocent he is. But if Arthur loves Pierre, what difference does all the rest make? Pierre has already forgotten all his rage. He asks: "You're sure he cares for me?"

"Listen, kid," Lucas replies, "why don't you drop Bruggle and his shirts and his piss-elegant dressing gowns? Shack up with a nice young female. A few good fucks and everything will be OK. All right? For tonight, we'll steer you into something nice. After that, you turn in. A little snooze, and tomorrow, no problem. We'll walk you home. Where do you live?"

"Nowhere. I walked out on my mother today."

"OK, then you sleep at my place. I'll fix a bed for you in the study."

"Thanks, Lucas. I'd like that."

Lucas notes: "We're not far from Negrito's. I'm going there to see a pal of mine, a little black girl. Want to come?"

Pierre and Lucas at Negrito's. They no sooner cross the threshold than a dancer, her skin the color of black pearl, asks, "What about your American friend? Why isn't he with you tonight?" Your American friend. Arthur again. Always Arthur. Can't Pierre walk ten paces without finding the same shadow everywhere? He'd rather see Lucas in Hell than sit here listening to him praise this inquisitive picaninny, explaining how she's only fifteen, and he adores her, her name is Djamilina, etc., etc...But why think of Djamilina as a savage? Just a little girl drunk, she spreads her legs, bumps and grinds, throws a glance, then a hand, then her whole body at the man her child's whim has picked out for the night. Djamilina imagines she is on top of the world, just like a certain young man who was bragging about his freedom. Freedom. What are you doing with your freedom, Monsieur Arthur? A little hustler lies next to you in your bed, motionless. Monsieur Arthur and his little hustler. They must be asleep already, like a waxwork couple. If unconscious, they have begun to die. There's your freedom, Monsieur Arthur. One day Pierre will no longer exist for you nor you for Pierre. In the meantime, to keep one's patience, the thing to do is drink. Lucas looks as pale as a sheet, Djamilina exaggerates the gratuitous lewdness of what she is doing with him. Djamilina, a cruel doll, and Bruggle, that toy one can use so long before realizing how many vicious possibilities are stored up inside its clockwork. May tonight's sleep turn Bruggle into stone. He'll still wake up, tomorrow, to fresh ravages. Tonight Diane weeps, thanks to Pierre, and Mme. Dumont-Dufour poisons herself with rage. Nowhere on earth is there peace for the living. Before going to sleep one ought to take one's heart out of one's body, like removing a wallet from a jacket breast pocket. But, because one can't, these things are all a sham. Dance, Djamilina, and as for you, Mr. Sound-Mind-in-a-Sound-Body, who just gave me such good advice about my sex life, go ahead and suffer! Djamilina is just a kid. At four A.M. she's sorry she can't spell. "Teach me some grammar," she asks, her hand suddenly very busy on Lucas' fevered thighs. Pierre watches her wrist move up and down. Now her nails are digging into the material. She's hurting him, he shoves her away, she falls, she screams, she cries, he drags her away to the washroom in an effort to calm her down.

Pierre, alone at the table, drinks the rest of the champagne straight from the bottle. He does not wait for the couple to come back, reconciled. "Waiter, my hat and coat, please!" Then he leans over to ask, "Are you leaving with me, Arthur?" There is no reply. Pierre remembers...Arthur, the little hustlers...Let's go, then.

DIFFICULT DEATH

Keep a stiff upper lip. Tonight Arthur's freedom is Totor. What about Pierre's? The door slides open. Three cheers for the street. An all-night drugstore.

Pierre knows the exact dosage of sleeping pills to take in order never to wake up.

He goes straight to the drugstore.

Already, from the display window, little green, red, violet, and yellow bottles, butterflies of death, brush past him.

He goes inside, buys the medication, walks out with it clenched in his fist, and hurries to an empty avenue where there are benches.

He lies down, swallows eight capsules, crosses his hands over his coat, and lets the night enter his bones.

Night, cold, death, freedom.

His mind goes back...Once before, alone in the midst of a great void, a boy with a hollow body was confronted by two eyes. There was nothing left anywhere but those two eyes. Diane's eye, precise, sad, and of a self-limiting awareness. Bruggle's eye, the most beautiful human eye Pierre has ever seen. A human eye but an animal eye as well, which love itself could never tame. Pierre begs both eyes to forgive him. He begs Diane to forgive him for having preferred the animal to the woman. But the beast Bruggle, boy savage, still has the grandeur of innocence, even in his cruelty. Arthur. A cold draft nothing can stop. Arthur is right and not Pierre, who is already mingled with the wood of the bench on which he lies. A throat without warmth, a mineral body, and a brain, a paltry flower of blood drying up in the window box of a skull. In the whole of the universe there are only two points in which feeling remains. Two eyes, Bruggle's and Diane's, already devoured by the night, moving closer together. Touching, they set the world on fire.

Chapter Five

A HELPING HAND

In the hospital where she came the next morning with Mme. Dumont-Dufour and her mother to identify a dead body, Diane saw a boy so handsome she thought she was weeping from admiration instead of grief.

The two mothers were at her side, upright in their black shawls, Mme. Blok, her eyes swollen with tears, Mme. Dumont-Dufour, scrawny and shriveled as ever, but as soon as she unbuttoned her lips, her voice was so false and cold, Diane suddenly realized the same comedy Pierre had deliberately stopped playing for her was one she intended to inflict on others. Will she never die and know that peace in which Pierre's face is frozen now? Diane chokes and falls across the dead child, all white in this room. Her arms cling to an already stony body, her mouth wanders over a face she is learning gradually to know no more.

She is going to have to be led out. Mme. Blok and Mme. Dumont-Dufour have grabbed one arm apiece, and have already reached the doorway with her, when the sight of a young boy on the threshold makes Diane blanch and pull up short, baring her teeth. But she no sooner pulls loose than she stops, for on the other's face she has seen tears like her own, tracing furrows of pain. Her lips are capable of just enough movement to murmur a name: "Bruggle."

Bruggle.

Draped in black silk and virtuous pride, the look of an exorcist in her eye, Mme. Dumont-Dufour sweeps out of the room. Mme. Blok does not venture to imagine that she has any other business

DIFFICULT DEATH

here than to follow a mother in her grief. So Diane and Bruggle are left alone. Because Diane sees a pair of hands whose beauty she had always thought merciless wrung with woe, in the name of the dead Pierre she pities Bruggle's sobs.

Now that Pierre is dead, this trans-Atlantic feline she has loathed until today, this creature of unalterable and diabolical innocence, weeps.

Diane hears his voice, pleadingly: "Diane, Diane, he was the only person on earth I ever loved, the only one I thought of when I was blue and down in the dumps, by myself in the studio. Diane, Diane, why did he die?"

Diane is not sure why she is going to live. She is not about to make any answer. She lets Bruggle come put his head on her shoulder, sobbing. Bruggle, she understands, is also a victim. A starstruck child. Pierre has told her a thousand times how Bruggle crossed the Atlantic in the hold of a ship. He was thin, poor, humble. He arrived, a boy savage, eyes as big as saucers, intoxicated at the idea he could arouse desire and passion in others, ambitious, uncompromising, haughty in his aspirations. Diane remembers how Pierre spoke of his love the first time. "The child Septentrion danced two days and pleased."

The child Septentrion. Bruggle has lost all his rhythm now. Pierre is dead. Bruggle falls on his knees, clasps his hands over a pair of cold hands, hands that reached for him in their dreams. Bruggle is all alone himself, now. Bruggle still asks: "Why, why was there such a passion in him that he was capable of believing I could do anything?"

Why was there such a passion in Pierre?

Diane feels despair rising in Bruggle like a floodtide of madness. Diane's fingers once more find a brow they would soothe with their caress. Diane, who neither could nor would condemn, even now holds out a helping hand.

Design by David Bullen
Typeset in Mergenthaler Joanna
by Walker & Swenson
Printed by Maple-Vail
on acid-free paper